THE GARDEN OF YOUTH

AGAINST ALL ODDS

Deborah Diamond Driskill

ISBN: 0990467201
ISBN 13: 9780990467205

ACKNOWLEDGEMENTS

To My everything, the Second Adam. The Scriptures tell us, so it is written: "The first man, Adam, became a living person. But the last Adam--that is, Christ—is a life-giving Spirit." *II Corinthian 15:45 New Living Translation Bible*

To my wonderful husband and best friend on Earth, Dwight Driskill, and to everyone instrumental in getting me to the place that I am at today. Thanks for your prayers. I love you all!

ENDORSEMENTS

The Garden of Youth is a masterpiece of literature. The author, who happens to be my beautiful and lovely wife, has done an excellent job in mesmerizing the reader. I was drawn into the story-line, and left in awe as the events unfolded differently than I had expected. You, the reader, will be captivated and mystified as you journey through the Garden of Youth. This literary work is extraordinary.

Dwight A. Driskill
Senior Pastor and Founder of God's Church of Miracles International

Deborah Driskill is an exciting new voice with a phenomenal imagination to draw youth out of the caverns of darkness into the light of God. In the melting pot of her creativity, the blend of spiritual reality with fiction shines through.

Dr. Janice Hurst
Dramatist/Personae` Psalmist
Author of *Snake in my Bosom*

In this book, Deborah Driskill challenges us all to develop a higher level of faith. If you are willing to trust God for the impossible, this book is for you.
Shirley A. Kyle
Pastor of Dominion Life Worship Center

Take your thought of redemption to a new level and read this book. Deborah Driskill uses an adolescent's journey to reveal God's ultimate plan for our lives.

Apostle Dennis S. Kyle
Founder and Overseer of Dominion Life Worship Center

TABLE OF CONTENTS

FOREWORD

The author, Deborah Diamond Driskill, has proven to be not only a phenomenal playwright, but an author like no other. Her writings are based on her deep love that she has for her heavenly Father, and being intimately involved with Him, she expresses His heart. She is anointed to hear His voice, and speaks loud and clear what she has heard. She is such a gifted woman of God, filled with passion for the healing and deliverance of young people. Her passion is to help release the captive from the torment of society. Her goal is to heal the broken-hearted, and set the captive free.

Being a devoted co-pastor with her loving husband, they have found the youth of their church to be their very own fountain of youth. Deborah uses nurturing skills to provide godly counsel for the future pastors, evangelists, teachers, preachers, missionaries, doctors, lawyers, business owners and parents. Her goal is to provide a positive role model that glorifies God, and that will in turn encourage them to become ambassadors for Christ.

Having suffered loss in her immediate family, Deborah receives healing by giving to the young-and they, in turn, bring restoration to her life. Her goal is to spend the rest of her life giving, and pouring out the love that she has been given. She is comforted in knowing that the youth trust her and her husband, and they appreciate what God allows them to do. If she can help a young person reach their highest goal in life, it makes her living worthwhile.

The creative writing in this novel draws you into every line and every page. Many young people will be intrigued by this work, and will want to know how it ends. This novel will help young people to make decisions that will benefit them for the rest of their lives. King Solomon says in the Scriptures: Get Wisdom (skillful and godly Wisdom)!... [For skillful and godly Wisdom is the principal thing.] And with all you have gotten, get an understanding (discernment, comprehension, and inter-pretation). This novel gives insight to the young and the restless.

Her motivation came one day when she had this thought: -what would it be like if there was a place that young people could go, without any adult supervision?-. My, what a ride she takes you on. After reading this book, young people will have a deep appreciation for the authority that has been placed over them.

This book was written out of blood, sweat and tears; the many attacks that took place only proves that Deborah is a survivor, and her desire is to help others to overcome the many life obstacles that come their way. Not only does she want to publish more books and produce more plays, she also wants to own her own publishing company where she can help others (especially young people) express themselves with the creative literary gifts that they possess.

Deborah is a writer with a heart that pleases God, a woman that is filled with love and compassion, the joy of the Lord is her strength. She is a woman who is wonderfully and fearfully made, and the strength that she has been given is expressed in this book. This is a book that we all can learn from, and the moral of the story is that we need God to lead and guide us into paths of righteousness.

Dr. Gloria Nicholson
Pastor/Founder of Glow Ministries
Author of two books, *Violated* and *Poems of Inspiration: Volumes I-IV*

PREFACE

This book describes an adolescent's journey into the world of the supernatural. The entrance into the Garden of Youth frees its occupants from parental admittance and authority. The garden itself is characterized as a paradise for every youthful desire imaginable, allowing young people to live as they choose.

The idea for the book was birthed as I sat in deep thought about our millennial youth of the world. What it would be like if they lived as a nation. Living out their rebellions, and fighting rejections in life. However, coming to their senses enough to leave the garden would inevitably bring about life-or-death consequences for each of them.

The Garden of Youth is not only mysterious in nature, but spiritually uplifting as well. We are all in need of guidance at some point in our lives. With rebellion at our heels and in our hearts to one degree or another, just like the characters in this book, we respond.

This is a good read for youths fourteen through twenty-one. It is trans-generational in nature. This literary work will travel from parents and their children to young adults and grandparents who are raising teenagers.

Some readers will be enriched while reading, to find out how good it can be to forgive someone. Even to love someone else through the pain and sufferings that they face in life. Others will remember what it was like when they struggled with their own rebellions and felt misunderstood. Prayerfully, those who read this book will come to the conclusion that submitting to positive authority is not such a bad idea after all.

The challenges I faced during my journey of writing brought me face to face with the Second Adam. Either I could finish the story, or leave it tucked away safely in a computer file.

Opening the file and finishing the book has awarded the Second Adam the opportunity to touch young hearts and revisit others. I am grateful in this time and season of my life to thank everyone who prayed for me when I asked the Second Adam-where are you in my life? I cherish every prayer and every seed of encouragement, and I thank you with all that is within me.

May you realize in the most difficult seasons of your life that He is the answer you need, and remember, it's only a season that you are contending with, and seasons do pass.

The first of many,

Deborah Diamond Driskill

CHAPTER ONE

It's My Way or No Way

Mom, it's Friday!" I moaned loudly.

"Allison! Watch your tone of voice with me, young lady!"

Mom threw the head of lettuce into the sink. It bounced from side to side before finding a good place to settle. I quickly softened my tone.

"So it's Friday. Should that mean something to me?" My Mom asked, raising an eyebrow at me.

"That's what I wanted to talk to you about."

"Oh?" She faced me, giving me her full attention.

"You're working the late shift."

"I leave in fifteen minutes." Mom looked at the clock and into my eyes, with her mind already made up.

"But Mom, I haven't asked you yet." Mom placed her hands on her hips and waited.

"Can I...may I invite a few friends over tonight? Please? What could it possibly hurt?" My plea dangled in midair under the unintimidating gaze of my strong-willed mother. I was convinced that she was determined to keep me, her daughter hostage until after high school graduation.

"Mom?" My eleven-year-old sister Meghan piped up, was ready to tell all. Her biracial features were offset by Mom's silky hair and green eyes. Though aggravating, her inner beauty still prevailed, just like Mom's. Mom swung her body toward the family room and craned her neck in the direction of the big-screen TV.

"Allie met a new friend at school."

"Oh she did, did she?" Meghan's head moved up and down faster than a bobble head toy.

She added,

"Mm-hmm, her friend's name is CayLeigh Stewart."

"Mind your own business!" I yelled in disgust.

"Mind your own business!" She mimicked.

"Watch your cartoons, Meghan!" I barked through closed teeth.

I rounded the corner of the kitchen island yelling in my defense. "Mom!" Mom thrust her finger at my sister's bedroom door. "Meghan, go! Go now! I am talking to your sister!" Meghan stomped her way down the hall to her bedroom. She slammed the door, reopened it, and gently closed it behind her.

"Mother, Meghan will be here with us, and you know yourself that she's worse than a news reporter. You just witnessed her in action." Mom continued to prepare the salad for her midmorning lunch, unaffected by my words. Dead silence dominated the conversation for two whole minutes.

"All right then. Will you consider letting me go to my friend's party tonight?"

"I need the cell phone numbers and email addresses of the adult chaperones."

"Oh, so now you don't trust me."

"Trust is earned. We've been through all this before." Mom drummed her fingers on the lid of the plastic container that she had put the salad in.

2

I flopped down in the chair next to the sliding glass door and rebelliously dangled my leg over the arm of her chair. Mom worked feverishly to make payments on it, and cared for it with the rigorous care she gave to all of her possessions. I knew which strings to pull. Hopefully this would work and she would drop me off at the party just to get me out of her hair.

"Allison Milan Flemings, get your leg off the arm of the chair!" Refusing to do so, I folded my arms in deep-seated anger and stared out the window. My little bug of a sister listened to everything that went on through the open crack of her bedroom door.

"A month's detention from the movies and your friends may convince you. Not to mention a month's worth of snacks." Without a response from me, she continued, "I'll save at least one hundred and fifty dollars this month from this grounding." I paid her no attention. She would hold it over my head, and use it again, if she knew she had shaken me with her words.

Meghan threw the door open and ran into our mother's arms. "Mommy, no! What goes for her goes for me too!" Meghan pleaded with every inch of her body.

"Go back to your room and finish your homework. You are safe as long as you obey house rules."
"Whew! Thank God." Meghan lifted her head and her hand and blew a kiss toward heaven. She knew without a doubt it had reached the cheek of Jesus. Meghan had a smile on her face and a skip in her step, when she closed the door behind her.

Just like Meghan, I realigned my focus. If finding a way to go to this party meant detentions for the next three months – then so be it! I could no longer put off giving CayLeigh my answer, considering the party would began within the next couple of hours.

Tears raced down my nose and splattered the ink on the invitation CayLeigh had given to me. For two weeks I had held onto it for dear life, hoping and praying for a chance to attend the party of a lifetime. I recalled the conversation with regret.

"All the other teens your age will be there." CayLeigh cajoled.

"Remember, I won't be sixteen until the day after Thanksgiving."

"Oh yeah, that's right." She held her head high. "No adolescent parties until your sixteenth birthday, unless it's a party for your little sister."

CayLeigh's laughter had rubbed me the wrong way that day. I immediately felt like a prisoner in my own home and could not wait to leave. If Cayleigh's mom was my mom, things would be different for me. CayLeigh's mom was an *anything-goes-mom*. It did not matter what it was. For that matter, defiance carefully inscribed those words on the center of my heart. I knew this was going to start trouble.

I neatly folded the invitation card and tucked it away where Mom would never find it: the velvet pink jewelry bag that held my butterfly diamond pendant. Dad had bought me the pendant against Mom's will, and he made me promise not to wear it until my sixteenth birthday. Mom thinks I gave it back. That was my first real big lie to her. It did not feel so bad. It had been easier than I thought it would be.

The lie meant peace between Mom and me, and that was just fine with me. She could not figure out why Dad would buy a five hundred and fifty dollar butterfly pendant necklace, when a new laptop computer was needed for my studies. Mom had the right to question Dad's motive. She always had my best interests at heart. It just took so long before I realized it.

When I held the pendant close to my heart, hot stinging tears surfaced in my eyes. The keepsake photo that we took together at the amusement park tumbled from the bag. It seemed like ages ago.

The camera lens had captured the undeniable love that Dad had for his family. Yet at the same time, childhood memories were fading fast and it was getting harder to remember our life together as a family.

I placed the keepsake photo and butterfly pendant safely in the jewelry bag. My leg slid down the arm of the chair with my feet resting on the floor. Before Mom could turn to face me, I started sobbing with my face buried in my hands.

Mom came over and caressed my hand as she kneeled beside the chair. "Honey, I love you and I have to do what's best for you."

"I just wanted a few friends over for a couple of hours. That's all."

"That won't happen unless I'm at home and that's final." Mom would not budge in changing her final answer, although she had been stern and kind in its delivery.

I braced myself for the lecture about our house rules. The house rules roared through my mind even when Mom was not thinking about house rules. They still echo in my memory after all this time. "We have higher standards in our home. You have to choose your friends wisely these days." Well, last and worst of all, "You must be home by 11pm, even on weekends."

A few of my friends laughed at me whenever Mom came to pick me up. It would not have been so bad if it had been Dad. Dad would do anything to make me happy. When we spent the night with his side of the family, my sister and I had a ball. The opportunity availed me to choose from a list of things I wanted to do, being the oldest. Mom believes it had happened that way because he occasionally took advantage of his visitation rights. It was more than that. We did not see him much but it was a daddy's love and Meghan and I would never forget it.

That night with Mom, yours truly would have done anything to leave the house. Meghan knew me well, and she knew I would work overtime to convince Mom about the party. She eased her way into the narrow hallway behind Mom's back so I could read her lips. "Hey Allie," she mouthed, "you're not going anywhere, loser!" She feigned punching herself in the face several times, and then dashed back to her room. Meghan got no response from me. I remembered the party.

"Meghan?"
"Yes, Mom?" She responded from her room.
"Are you behaving yourself?"
"Mom, I'm in my room." She replied.

Mom turned to me and our eyes locked. I leaned forward to peer into her soul, searching for a glimmer of hope that I might have weakened her a bit. The only thing visible in her eyes was myself...with red eyes from crying, jet black wavy hair and dark olive colored skin, we grimaced at each other with disappointment. Mom rose to her feet. "You seem to have forgotten I was fifteen once." She folded her arms and her body swayed with displeasure. "I will not allow you to manipulate me, Allison Milan Flemings."

"I want to go live with daddy."
"He's your father. I will not deny you if that's what you choose to do. We'll talk to him and work through it." It was clear to me that if my mother did not want me, surely my dad would warmly welcome me with open arms.

In the dining area, my overstuffed book bag lay humbly on the glass tabletop. I dragged the book bag across the glass tabletop with my keys still attached to it, and refused to look for scratches. The weight of the book bag swung over my shoulder and tipped my balance. After catching my balance, my shoes caught my peripheral vision. The immediate decision to pick up the shoes that had hit the wall, after I threw them across the room was a good one. Matters could get even worse, if Mom saw that side of my extreme teen outrage.

After gathering my belongings, my rebellion forced me to the sliding glass door, and onto the patio away from the rest of the family. When I slouched onto the lounger with my English Literature book, thoughts of Dad flickered through my mind. Carelessly flipping through the book's pages, my hunger for Dad's presence superseded all homework assignments.

Opportunity seldom arose to see Jason Flemings (a.k.a. Dad). However, when they did, I always jumped at the chance. We looked alike and acted alike and I was just as intellectually studious and defiant (though I only found that out years later).

Restless nights kept me awake thinking of ways to destroy his relationship with his girlfriend. The need to go to a movie with Dad alone for just once, was necessary. He needed to know about the young man that was slowly capturing my interest. CayLeigh Stewart knows nothing about this guy even though, she was quickly becoming my closest friend. He was five years my senior and this time Dad's presence was in demand.

Neighborhood noises surrounded our condominium. I angled my head toward the area of the confusion, but I could not see anything. The privacy wall and the four hedges that stood in a neat row prevented contact with the real world. Things remained the same concerning the hedges even though, my complaint about them coming down stood firm. It is okay though. Another eighteen months in this dump, then I am gone.

Plans unfolded in my mind like a cherry blossom opening to reveal its inner beauty on a perfect April morning. I met Mom in the kitchen and apologized to her for wanting to break the house rules. She stood in amazement at my lack of defiance, and was puzzled at what could have softened me.

"Mom, you work so hard to take care of us all by yourself. I'm sorry for the way I treated you. You deserve better." In the middle of our embrace, I believe Mom somehow felt betrayed by the kiss I planted on her cheek. She stood in the same spot for several minutes thinking about it.

From that moment on, my false act of surrender had been successful. I purred like a kitten and walked just as softly. I grabbed my cell phone, crammed my things back into my book bag and stood in the corner of the privacy wall to escape the cool autumn breeze that floated off Michigan's Rouge River.

The rest of my plan of operation went as smooth as clockwork. I had not spoken with my cousin in over a month. He missed me dearly. I arranged everything over the phone with Ian, and energy coursed through my veins after our conversation was over. Now it was time for phase three.

"Mom, don't worry about tucking Meghan into bed. I'll do it." Meghan lay on her stomach kicking her legs up and down. She allowed them to fall freely against the bed.

Meghan complained, "For God's sake, I'm eleven years old. I don't need my fifteen year old sister tucking me into bed."

Without a verbal response from me, I marched lovingly to the laundry room and searched the laundry basket on a mission. Meghan's black pajamas with the leopard print collar and cuffs lay scrunched down in the very bottom of the basket. I wildly shook the wrinkles out of the pajamas and rushed them to her room.

"Here Megh, put these on."

"I don't want to. I have my pink kitty jammies on." I smiled at my little sister and tried forcing her to take the pajamas. "I'm in the middle of my Playstation game."

"Pause it." I snatched the game control from her.

"Mom, make Allison leave my room!"

"No fair, Megh. I don't want you to get cold during the night, that's all."

Mom entered the war zone. "I heard you from my room. Your sister's room stays warm, Allison."

"Yes, Mom. I forgot." She planted a kiss on each forehead and headed to the closet to get her coat.

"You'll put these on before the night is over." Those words were spoken to my young sibling with the utmost confidence that it would happen. Meghan caught the pajamas and threw them over the footboard of the bed with an attitude. My smile and cordiality followed Mom down the hall to the small open foyer leading to the front door.

"Take care of things, honey."

"I will. You can trust me, Mom."

"I'll call you on my lunch hour to check on you, okay?" She pulled her hat down over her ears.

"Okay, Mom. I'm going to hop in the shower while Meghan is playing her game, then I'll order pizza just like you said."

"That sounds good. I love you."

"I love you too."

Mom closed the door and drove off. I peeked through the blinds, hoping that Ian remembered his cue was Mom's need for a new brake light. Maybe his *dopiness* would not make him miss it. After all, Mom had devoured the tender bait that I had offered her. Mom swallowing the bait hook, line and sinker had made me a happy camper. Now it was time to follow through with the second half of phase three.

CHAPTER TWO

Mission Accomplished

The front doorbell rang. Meghan stared at the door. Why did Meghan stare at the door? It was her response to house rule number four: only I could answer the door if Mom was not around. "Who is it?" she asked. She eventually walked back to her room, with silence as her only answer after several attempts.

The neighbor's Doberman Pinscher's endless barking lured Meghan to the window. The gentle tap on the patio glass door made her aware of the shadow that had been peering in from the darkness. She took a closer look. "Ian, what are you doing out there? And why are you dressed in all black? You look like a robber."

He thrust himself inside and placed his hand over her mouth. "Shh! Between you and Mr. Fontaine's dog, you have the potential to wake up the entire community! Has Aunt Janet left for work yet? I was looking for her car."

"Yes, but what are you doing here?" Ian tried smiling to mask his fear.

"I decided to come over and check on you and Allison. Is there anything wrong with that?"

"No. I'm glad to see you. You're my favorite cousin, you know."

"So sorry I can't say the same about you, Megh."

"It's okay. I like you anyway."

"You are so naive." he said.

She fluttered her eyelashes and leaned her face against prayer hands and replied, "So are you," without understanding the meaning of the word he had just spoken.

All eyes fell on me when I entered the room. "Hey," Meghan exclaimed, "you're dressed in all black too. What are you two up to?"

"Shut up and put these on!" The pajamas flew across the room and into Meghan's arms.

The pajamas dropped to the floor. "But I—."

"Do what I said."

"Are you two going somewhere?"

Ian's display of nervous energy picked up the pajamas. "Megh, just put them on, okay?" He towered over her.

"You look nervous, Ian."

"Who, me? No, I'm good."

In Mom's room, her makeup and jewelry box awaited me. The small gold loop earring I fished for was leaning against the corner of the box. Reaching for the earring, Grandma Rachel's 1940 hat pin dug into my flesh. Startled by its prick, the jewelry box flipped out of my left hand and onto the bed. Four drops of blood formed a tiny circle on the tip of my index finger. I comforted my finger by gnawing on it after finding the earring.

The key ring that lay in the middle of Mom's bed struck my eye. Sharp pointed edges surrounded the medallion that hung from it. Mom's jewelry box was mine. However, the medallion was unfamiliar to me. I removed the smudge from the medallion's glass with the hem of my blouse, and took a closer look. A piece of a fish's eye stared back at me from beneath the medallion's glass. It winked at me and I started feeling woozy. I placed it back where I found it, and quickly left the room.

"Hey Allison, I don't know how good of an idea this is." Ian leaned against the bedroom door with Meghan's pajamas wadded in a ball. "Megh won't change her pajamas."

"She will when I get through with her!"

"I don't think it's such a good idea to go to the party."

"Why?" He searched for his answer. I snatched the pjs from him and rushed him down the hall.

"You are so chicken-hearted!"

Muffled cries escaped Meghan's room with her head buried beneath the pillow. "Meghan, what's wrong?"

"You're acting sneaky again, Allison."

"Think about it, Megh. It's just that the only person we can ride to the store with is Ian. You know that's all right with Mom."

Ian braved up. "Y-yeah, what's so sneaky about that?"

Meghan sat up for a moment to think about that. "Mom does trust you so I guess I do too." She dried her eyes. Ian whimpered like a frightened puppy under his breath, and lowered his head. She changed her pajamas and the three of them loaded in the car.

Ian stopped at the convenience store to load up on bite-sized snacks. He gave them all to Meghan to quiet her. Even with the candy, questions ran from Meghan like water from a faucet with a broken handle.

"What have I gotten myself into?" he whispered underneath Meghan's questions.

I switched on the radio. "Ian, it's not impossible for you to have a good time."

"What about Meghan?"

"I told you already, they have a sitting service."

"A sitting service at a party? Are you sure?"

"That's what CayLeigh said."

"Cay...Leigh? I'm dead. I'm completely dead when Aunt Janet finds out. My favorite aunt is going to kill me."

"I have to use the bathroom. I can't hold it much longer." Meghan tapped her feet against the floor board of the car.

"Just give us a minute to park."

"I have to go now!" My threats slapped her face, so I would not have to. I had ways of inflicting pain that left no bruises, but my heaviest artillery was used only on rare occasions.

Ian gazed at the height of the building. "I don't remember this hotel being this tall before."

"Think about it Ian. It's been years since our family celebrated our last reunion here. We were little then."

"What about me?" Meghan asked.

"You were just a baby. Mom and Dad were together then."

"Huh?" Ian stopped walking and scratched his head. "That doesn't make any sense. Since we're older shouldn't the building look smaller?"

"Hey, he's right." My venomous gaze silenced them both, as we entered the building.

We walked down the long corridor and boarded the elevator in silence. After a matter of seconds, the elevator jerked abruptly to a standstill. Sharp squeals escaped Meghan's pursed lips. A sharp pain seized my neck, and I pressed into it with my thumb to ease the pain that settled between my shoulder blades. Ian had held onto the railing tighter than he would have if he were on a ride at an amusement park. We slowly gathered our disheveled bodies together and waited for the doors to open.

I announced our arrival. "Well, here it is room 777."

CHAPTER THREE

Admittance at Any Cost

Y ou are in big trouble, Allison." Meghan's ploy of intimidation had no
ground to stand on.

"Shut up! I don't need lip from you right now."

"I'm afraid."

"Well, don't be!"

"It's not too late to leave." Meghan whispered.

"Megh is right." Ian's eyes glazed over with fear.

"Oh no... you look just like daddy right now, and that means we're
walking through that door." Meghan took Ian by the hand and pulled
him close.

"Go on Ian," Urging him with force to knock on the door, he said,
"It's your party. You knock." They took their places behind me and
pushed me closer to the door.

The doorknocker's thud reverberated down the hall. "Let's go." Ian
pleaded. "Hotel doors are equipped with peepholes, not door knock-
ers." He hooked his arm in mine to pull me away.

The door panel lit up when the automated voice spoke. "Admission
is three. Is that right?"

Meghan backed away screaming each word. "No! Admission is one!
Admission is Allie!"

Ian turned away from the door with Meghan at his heels. "We'll wait for you in the car."

"Freeze! Get back here!" The power in my voice compelled them. They backed up slowly, and executed an about-face in front of the door.

An oversized handprint suddenly appeared on the wall to the left of the door. The light impulses inside it carried red liquid throughout the handprint, almost looking like blood vessels. Shafts of light radiated from the center, forming the outline of the hand and its fingers. I stepped forward to place my hand on the scanner.

"Ian." The automated voice spoke for the second time. "Place your hand on the scanner first. Meghan will follow you. Then of course it will be your turn, Allison. After all, you are the reason that they are here." We obeyed the automated voice, astonished that it knew our names.

Ian placed his hand fearlessly inside the oversized palm. It shrunk to the size of his hand. Ian felt a surge of courage knowing that he was being admitted as one of CayLeigh Stewart's guests. Meghan stood behind him for her turn. Instantly the hand moved its position to match her height. The image of the hand shrank to conform to the size of Meghan's hand. It repeated its course with me.

The door opened slowly, seemingly trying to give us time to change our minds. At least, that was the impression that I got. It made me all the more curious. The eighteen-year-old who manned the door stuck his head through the crack just enough to peek. He checked me out first, and then my little sister. Meghan would not have survived if looks could kill.

"I don't see how you were admitted into an everlasting party with her." In pride, my peacock chest took the lead. "I am CayLeigh Stewart's closest friend." "Too bad she doesn't know that." He opened the door for us to enter and I sneered at him as we walked past.

The room was packed with people - no one else could possibly fit inside the room. The air was thick and stale. Music was blaring so loudly the windows rattled. People had to yell to talk to each other and strained to hear. "Meghan, stay close to me. I don't want to have to look for you." She placed her hand in mine, and extended her other hand to Ian. Now we were in a dangerous situation in the overcrowded room. Meghan forced her words out. "I can't breathe!"

Suddenly, the walls expanded to accommodate the crowd as they moved around. Now there was plenty enough space for everyone. The surroundings were no longer that of a hotel suite. It had become one big dimly lit windowless square room, with a hallway leading into darkness and one door for entry. Everyone cheered at this marvel, except for the three of us. Meghan's eyes were as big as saucers, and Ian nearly fainted. Meghan's big sister was no better. I felt the blood drain from my face, and I froze in my tracks when the walls expanded.

Shaken by this strange phenomenon, we began our search for CayLeigh, and asked bystanders if they had seen her. The forty to fifty strangers there greeted us, but no one knew who CayLeigh was. However, their comments and small talk proved that they knew who we were. At this point, Ian was beside himself, and Meghan was extremely upset and needed to find a bathroom immediately. By this time, my mind was made up into going back home as soon as my sister relieved herself.

We walked past the front door again on our way to the bathroom. A couple of boys cornered Ian about some magazines he had read prior to coming to the party. I could not help him out at the time. We left him to dig his way out of that one. I mouthed to him that we would stop by on our way out the door.

"There's the bathroom. Go." Meghan rushed to the bathroom door with her snacks in her hand. The door flew open and five little girls

Meghan's age moved her out of the way. They giggled as they skipped down the hallway into the darkness. We watched the hallway disappear as quickly as it had appeared.

"Allison, did you see—?"
"Hurry up, so we can go home!"

The laughter of the little girls followed her into the bathroom. The door nearly closed behind Meghan before I could enter, but sticking my foot inside the door kept it from closing. I watched the laughter spiral to the ceiling and spread throughout the room. It took up physical space and used up the oxygen in the room. She lifted her eyes in the direction of the laughter that hung over her head. The laughter bounced her tiny frame all over the room, but she managed to free herself long enough to make it to the door. Living laughter pushed her away before she could reach the door knob. Her arm hit the lid of the toilet, and her hand struck the handle, flushing it. I reached for her hand. The water gurgled so loudly she plugged her ears with her fingers. Its force tugged at her pajamas pants and held the door securely against my foot.

The water force drew her closer and closer to the edge of the toilet. She struggled to breathe. When the door flew open the water force lifted her up, and down into the toilet. The laughing voices jumped into the commode after her. She swirled around and around and around. I reached my hand inside the toilet hardly touching her fingertips, but it was too late. It was like fighting to keep her head above water without actually being under water.

There were lots of adolescents that zoomed through that wet tunnel with Meghan. But she was the only one that made it to the entrance, finally swirling onto solid ground. Meghan lay face-down on a grassy green knoll, with her arms and legs sprawled out. Her insides swayed dizzily as she lay, continuing to react to the swirling motion. Her body flipped and flopped like a fish out of water until normalcy finally returned.

I screamed until I was hoarse. "Whoever you are, whatever you are, take me too!" The water force whistled. My eyes burned and my face stung from the tears that saturated my cheeks. "Please!" My little sister can't take care of herself!" The water force roared which made me think it was communicating with me. I knew for sure that it was, when it pushed me out of the bathroom and onto the floor. I wallowed in front of the bathroom door. The door slammed shut. I jumped to my feet to reach for the doorknob. It dissolved before my very eyes.

I fled from the scene searching for Ian, desperate for help. He would know what to do. "Oh God, I must find Ian!" Hearing those words aloud meant it was time to get Ian and find my baby sister to go home.

Just when I thought the situation could not get any worse, I arrived at the spot where we agreed to meet Ian. How could I meet Ian at the front door, if there was no front door? My face was on fire with perspiration, and hot tears stung my eyes as I stared at the blank wall. Stomach cramps took over the moment. What had I done? Where were my sister and cousin?

The young men that were with Ian earlier were on the opposite side of the room. The larger one stood with his arms folded, and the toe of his shoe resting on the floor. A sly smile crossed his face. His slender friend's idiotic grin mirrored his, and his upper body swayed almost uncontrollably. I backed off my approach, when I saw the evil that masked their faces. In backing away, strong slender fingers grabbed my shoulders that pinned me to a standstill. Ian took my hand, and we headed in the opposite direction.

A mural of a little girl standing in a valley hung in place of the window where the guys had stood. She was looking at a huge mountain and tears streamed down her chubby cheeks. She looked exactly like Meghan at the age of four. "Look!" Ian pondered. He bumped my arm.

"D-do you see the tears streaming down her cheeks?" he asked. Tears from her eyes had fallen onto the front of his shirt. He gawked at the mural and then at his shirt.

"Hey, Ian!" The stick figure blundered behind him. "Ian, what are you doing here?"

Ian gathered his thoughts and turned to face the young man. "I'm looking for my cousin. We're leaving."

"We've been here long enough." He ignored my reply.

"Who is she?" The stick figure asked. "Is she your girl?"

"Yuck! She's my cousin, Roderick!"

Roderick shrugged. "By the way, you remember Tyler from school."

"The party hasn't even started yet." Tyler ranted.

"Nice to meet you, but it's time for us to go." Tyler glanced at me and dismissed my presence.

"Ian, are you able to speak for yourself?"

"Tyler, I wouldn't go if I didn't want to."

"At least give me the titles of some good reading material before you leave." He stood as close to Ian as he could.

"Back off, Tyler. Let's go!" Ian laid his hand on my back.

"There, there, sweetheart." Roderick moved Ian away from Tyler and me and walked him to the library across the hall. "Just give me a few suggestions before you leave."

Ian pulled away from Roderick. "I'm looking for my cousin. It's past her curfew."

"You should have thought about that before you came." He backed him into the room, where a group of avid readers surrounded him and crowded him against the bookshelf.

What I saw next was unbelievable. The bookshelf turned into a gigantic book and focused on Ian. I rushed through the crowd, trying to pull them away from him. Suddenly the book opened and inside it stood a giant bookworm, complete with its graduation cap and eyeglasses magnifying its red eyes.

The worm opened its gaping mouth, and the crowd rushed Ian. I continued to brave my way to him, but it was too late. Four of the readers hoisted his body in front of the worm and the worm struck. His upper body disappeared inside the bookworm's mouth. Upon a second gulp, my cousin had completely disappeared inside it. I fainted at the foot of the giant book as it slammed shut.

When I came to, I was standing in front of a sculpted cave in a room marked *The Apprentice Sculptures*. The art in the cave astounded me. My name appeared on the stand of an unfinished piece of work.

A small pebble bounced against the side of my shoe. It was part of a small trail of pebbles that led to a small mound. The rocky mound reached the foot of a gigantic mountain. Trying to make sense of my surroundings made no sense to me at all. I asked myself how such a huge mountain could possibly dwell inside of a building. I had no answer. The rock walls completely surrounded me without an exit in sight. The only way out was to climb the mountain. Everything I needed to scale it, lay at the foot of the mountain in front of me.

I tied the rope around my waist and felt the rock face. My first few steps were somewhat tentative. Nevertheless, the rock climb at the local Mall had been steeper than this one. That thought gave me courage, although that climb took place a couple of years ago. Before long, my experience had become an exhilarating upward climb. Careful foot placement and counting each step had become my every thought.

Excitement carried me, until I looked down and saw the gaping dark hole I had just crawled out of. In my devastation, I looked up for refuge. The dark clouds that hovered over the mountain began to spread down it. I heard them coming. The sound of the darkness crashed into me and I lost my footing. I fell, and spiraled into the deep darkness.

Hands reaching from the darkness pulled at me. I screamed for God, convinced that He could help. The hands stopped reaching for me at the mention of His name. The tumbling stopped amid the darkness, and my body hit the ground feet first. I hesitated to open my eyes, not knowing what awaited me.

CHAPTER FOUR

Choco Valley

Birds sang overhead and enjoyed the blue sky. Quiet sniffles filled the air.

"Meghan." My eyes flew open.

I would recognize my little sister's sniffles anywhere. I pushed myself up from the ground, and made a full circle searching for her.

Meghan's hands were covering her face. I walked gingerly toward her, and softly spoke her name. She threw herself into my arms and held on for dear life. Her wet hair clung to my lips. She shivered in relief.

"Is it really you? I thought I would never see you again."

"I got us into this, and I'll get us out."

"Have you seen Ian?"

"He was swallowed by a bookwo—."

"What?"

"Never mind."

"You were going to say he was swallowed by a bookworm, weren't you?!"

"Megh, we'll find him."

"How do you know?"

"I found you, didn't I?... Listen. I remember how we got here. And I'm guessing the bookworm is how he got here. We will find him." She nodded her head, squeezed my hand and walked away from me.

"Where do you think we are?"

"I don't know, but I am definitely ready to leave."

Pitiful groans floated from beyond the trees. We quickly rushed to the scene to see Ian struggling to his feet, with his glasses half-cocked on his face. We held each other for the longest time.

Our heads were still buried in the group hug, when we suddenly noticed a huge group of teenagers creeping upon us from every direction. We were ready to run, but it appeared that every nation around the world had surrounded us. Red, yellow, black, white and brown skins were united together as one race of their own. They were obviously on guard, and ready to defy any adult who would dare enter the garden.

"Who are you, and why have you come to the Garden of Youth?" The tribal leader of the teens glared at us. His walk over to me disturbed Ian and Meghan. I did not flinch. It was obvious that he considered me a threat to his leadership and the residents of the garden. Why, I did not know.

"I'm Allison, and this is my sister Meghan." Pointing at Ian, he nodded. "And this is my cousin Ian." Ian nodded and glared back at the leader, hiding his fear as best he could.

"We went to a party and ended up here." I thought that if I was honest with him and told the truth, he would help us get back home.

"I'm Charles, the commander of the entrance of the garden. And we are well guarded." The crowd roared with approval. "All right people tell the newcomers why they are here!"

The residents spoke as one. "The garden is a paradise party that never ends. Parents enter at their own risk. And youth that attempt to leave suffer the consequences."

Charles slid his thumbs in his pockets, swaggering. "These girls," he put his fingers between his teeth and summoned them with a whistle, "are Sasha and Halo, our attendants. They will take care of you, Allison and Meghan. Ian, you will follow me. I see great potential in you."

Meghan inched closer to me. "The little one doesn't look the type." One of the residents remarked.

"She needs backbone." Another yelled.

"I don't want to party. I want to go home." Meghan pleaded. The residents pressed in closer. Random comments were hurled at her from the crowd. "We will teach you how to have fun." "You'll be just like us."

"We will work with you to make it happen!"

Charles changed his tactics, apparently wanting to win Meghan over. He touched the tip of her chin and I moved his hand away before Ian could react. He said to Meghan. "You'll have so much fun, you'll forget that parental rules ever existed."

Charles cast his eyes upon a beautiful girl Meghan's age. She gave a tearful smile. My sister sidled up to the preteen who had also been forced into the garden by her older sister. "You don't look happy to me."

"You are quite mistaken. I am very happy and well pleased with the Garden of Youth." She turned away from Meghan.

"A-are you hungry?" She tossed the words over her shoulder to Meghan.

"Do you have a name?" Meghan retorted. Hoots resounded within the crowd. Charles motioned with his hand for two of his garden officials.

"Asa, Miles." They stepped forward. Intimidation flushed her face. "My, my name is Amaiya. I'm your tour guide." Charles addressed the crowd. "The girl speaks with hesitation. This calls for a replacement. How 'bout it, Meghan?" Asa and Miles took their place on both sides of Amaiya to escort her away.

"Amaiya, that's such a pretty name and you're such a lovely girl." Meghan said. The crowd flooded Meghan with insults and derision, but she stood her ground. She moved Asa and Miles' hands away from Amaiya and stood in front of her. The crowd exploded, and wanted to take matters into their own hands. They rushed toward Meghan, and held me and Ian back. Charles lifted his hands to halt the plans of the residents. The crowd backed down and began to dissipate, quelled by Charles' force of will.

Meghan's words and actions had clearly warmed Amaiya's heart. No one could compliment like Meghan. She was genuinely pure and sincere, just like Mom. From that moment on, Amaiya welcomed Meghan as her friend in the garden. She thanked my sister, and we followed her to fruit trees laden with rotting fruit. Seconds later, we passed a grove of fruit trees that bore no fruit. That's where the path ended.

The aroma that spread from the valley was alluring. Ian sniffed. "It couldn't be." Ian's neck stretched further than a swan's. He sniffed with all his might. "Is, is that chocolate I smell?" Some of the trees had branches with bars of chocolate hanging from them, and others had snacks like chips.

"Well, here's dinner!" Amaiya announced. "You can eat anything in the land without being hassled by your parents."

"What?" Ian asked.

"That's what the Garden of Youth is all about."

Meghan loaded the shopping bag that Amaiya gave her with as many candy bars and chips as she could handle. Ian was running from tree to tree like a madman. Aunt Jennifer had always punished him by taking his chocolate from him for a week or two. He loved chocolate more than anyone else I knew.

Ian was hypnotized after a third sniff. He leaped off a nearby ledge and rolled down the hill. Meghan followed. I stepped closer to the edge to take a look. Suddenly, my desire for chocolate soared and I lost all control. I ended up at the bottom of the valley floor on my behind, with Amaiya waiting to lift me up by my elbows.

Amaiya announced in a sing-song voice, "Welcome to Choco Valley, the Valley of Chocolate." We followed the aroma that the chocolate dished out.

To my left, chocolate-covered raisins in the raisin patch were the size of watermelons. The patch of chocolate malt balls next to the chocolate raisin vines quickly became Ian's favorite. Ian jumped over the fence, and searched the patch for the largest malt ball he could find. We invented a new game on the spot and began to play. Ian rolled the bowling ball-sized malt ball down the short path to the lemon drop bushes. The ball collided with the bush and lemon drops flew everywhere. Meghan moved faster than Ian and gathered three times as many drops and won.

Amaiya roared with laughter at the sight. However, her laughter faded as she remembered where she was. Our eyes met and she spoke with haste. "We must be swift in getting to the ponds." "Why?" I asked.

"The ponds are likely to be empty before sunset but after that, the scuffles can go on all night." And another thing."

Meghan spoke up. "We're listening."

"Remember the shortcut. It will come in handy." Another "why?" escaped my lips. She mapped out the directions by pointing her finger. "It will take you to the west side of the garden. Make sure you go to the right on the pathway."

Trees lined the path on both sides that we were on, and their thick branches created an arch above it. A small opening awaited us at the end of the trees.

Amaiya ran through the brush like a little warrior. Meghan tried to follow, but kept stumbling. Eventually Amaiya coached my sister, and the two soon disappeared ahead of me and Ian. Ian was pouring with sweat - his long ostrich legs were getting him nowhere. I stayed behind with him to help him along the way.

Finally, Ian and I reached the end of the trail. The last couple of tree limbs revealed an open path. The open path led us to several ponds where long lines of people waited for their favorite beverages. The cola ponds were most popular, and the fruit punch was second in demand. For certain, the lemon-lime and orange soft drinks were considered stomach settlers after too much candy.

We talked to some of the teenagers, and learned that the no swimming allowed signs were posted by the male machos in the garden. They fought to rule everything. The machoramas had met their match though. The nerds, (known as the nerdiacs), that lived on the other side of the swamp feared nothing.

Amaiya and several others gave warning of rival gang wars that took place on the south side of the garden. "You arrive there at your own risk." She warned, as we continued our tour of the grounds.

"Stay together," Amaiya advised as we walked through the court-yard of several apartment complexes. "We're passing through EMD quarters."

"That doesn't make sense." Meghan commented. "Chocolate we understand, but EMD quarters?" Ian nodded, and raised his eyebrows inquistively.

"It will." That's when we saw were they gathered.

"Oooh," Ian grinned. "EMD must stand for every male's dream, every healthy male's dream!"

Boys were everywhere. They were in the valleys, yelling from the mountaintops, swimming, climbing trees and making bungee jumping cords. Amaiya told us that the girls who lived nearby were always on guard, particularly after dark. Still, I must admit, being there was fun, and Mom was not in the garden on my back about the chores.

The revving up of the race cars forced Meghan into Ian's arms. That was the first pleasant fright she had encountered in the garden. Screams poured from the bleachers of the basketball fans. Ian headed for the court, until he heard the roar from the football stadium. He was undecided about which event to attend until … the busses pulled up.

Ian furrowed his forehead and knuckled his eyes at the sight of the beautiful girls. Girls had been bussed in from the northern part of the garden. "Look at the girls! Aw man, have you ever seen such enticement on two legs?" He closed his eyes and exhaled. Ian wiped the steam from his glasses and planted them securely back on his face. I steered Meghan away from the crowd of hungry males that were gawking at us as well.

By now the sun was going down, and the twilight refined the beauty of the garden. Ian had gotten caught up with the partygoers that lived above the valley, and we decided to look for him in the morning. The partiers had obviously prepared themselves for an all-nighter, and they wholeheartedly believed in the saying, "the more the merrier". Those who had suffered stricter parental guidance stood out like a sore thumb – they were there to change their ways from shyness to slyness. After all, not one person in the nation of youth could be trusted. However, the shy ones would soon be as the others.

CHAPTER FIVE

The Kind Stranger

After a while in the garden my views changed. When guilt surfaced I blamed myself for everything. The responsibility for Meghan and Ian being in the garden taunted me. They were innocent. My manipulations had positioned them there. To worsen the situation, we had not seen Ian in a couple of months and we did not know where to look. Even with all the chaos and activity taking place in the garden, Meghan still held onto the bag of snacks Ian had bought for her on our fateful car ride to the party.

Tears filled my eyes every time I saw the bag. It was a reminder of the night, we had pulled into that hotel parking lot. Hatred filled my heart for the things I had done to get us there. Regret ravished my soul, tormenting me night and day.

Amaiya led the way. She parted through the boys as if they did not matter. Meghan and I entered the cabin looking for the nearest bathtub. The other seven bunks were empty – obviously the others had not made it in yet. It was exactly one o'clock in the morning. According to Amaiya, their plan was to meet us tomorrow afternoon.

Meghan's pajama pants somehow appeared a couple of inches shorter than they had been when we entered the garden. Seeing this, more humiliation washed over me for having become a resident of the garden, and of having brought my sister with me. How long we had been there was hard to tell. The sun shone of its own accord most of the time. Some days were longer than usual. I caught the single tear that fell from my eye before it wet my cheek, and predicted our stay in the garden as having been close to eight or nine months.

Meghan stumbled to the side of her bed and collapsed to her knees. She stayed in that position for almost five minutes. That whole time, Amaiya did not take her eyes off her.

"What is she doing?"
"She's saying her prayers."
"Why aren't her lips moving?"
"Get up, I need your help."
"Why?"
"She's asleep." Amaiya chuckled at the sight of Meghan on her knees asleep with drool oozing from the corner of her mouth.

On the count of three we hoisted my sister's body up and onto the top bunk.

At one point, I dropped my end and Amaiya giggled. Meghan's hair nearly swept the floor, and her arms were splayed to and fro. Amaiya had already dragged the lower half of Meghan's body onto the bed before I managed to lift her torso back up.

"Allison, may I ask you a question?"
"What is it, Amaiya?"
"You're ready to go home, aren't you? Is it really that bad here?"
"That's two questions."
"Come on, Allison." I was ready, yes ready to blast her with heartfelt sarcasm. It was time for her to meet the real me.

However, the longing in her eyes drew me in. Somehow my robotic "Yes" summoned her to my bedside. I lifted the sheet and she crawled in next to me. She was beautiful, yet so lonely.

"How did you get here, Amaiya? I mean, to the garden?" She leaned her cheek against my shoulder and I leaned my head against hers, waiting for an answer. The soft hum of her breathing mixed with the sounds of the night like clockwork, and she had fallen asleep.

I eased out of bed with both girls fast asleep, into the cool, exhilarating morning air. Feeling helpless in my shame, I had not prayed in four years. Mom thought my connection to the teens at church was legitimate, but it was all an act. My interests lie in the pizza parties and activities without Meghan.

I leaned against a tree and cried until there were no tears. Even in the darkness the hand that suddenly caressed my shoulder did not startle me. It actually felt very comforting.

"Allison." He said. I placed my hand on top of His.
"Yes."
"Why are you crying? Isn't freedom from responsibility what you've always wanted?"
"I didn't know it was going to be like this. I want to go home."
"You do know it will be a fight to go back?" Standing in silence, He turned me to face Him. His familiarity stood out to me – I was sure I knew Him. I was very conscious of things He did not approve of. I always made Him a part of my outer circle. I never took the time to really get to know Him.

As He spoke, my mother's face swirled around in His. He was staring right at me, ensuring that I was truly listening to His every word. His hands looked like my grandmother's hands, stretched out toward me to comfort me. His ears looked like my grandpa's. Grandpa had always been eager to listen to what his little Sassy-Fras had to say.

"Are you sure you want to go back home? There are rules to follow if you do decide that's the place for you."

"Where else could I go? I'm not even seventeen yet."

"There's always your Dad, and his girlfriend Gwendolyn. Oh yes, and his mother, and her new husband Stanley."

My look of surprise did not catch Him off-guard at knowing their names. "It's okay to visit, but that atmosphere is not like home."

"There. You said it yourself. That's really narrowing the scope of where you can live. If you compromise your character, you can rent an apartment with CayLeigh."

"How do you know her? Nobody else here knows her." His eyes pierced deep within my heart. Even His silence spoke loud and clear to me. The stranger's compassion for CayLeigh and me brought tears to my eyes. Our actions and the consequences of those actions could be deadly for us. His very presence made me want to change. I could no longer look Him in the eye.

I inhaled the beauty of the valley. The river behind us gurgled peacefully as it zigzagged its way through the Garden of Youth. Strands of hair licked my face from the gentle breeze that enveloped us. The garden grounds were incredibly diverse – tropical, country, jungle, mountainous and prairie environments all rolled into one. It was gorgeous. There were bodies of water to suit any personality.

The narrow path we followed led us to a band of trees. When my foot touched the ground, the trees parted and the white sands of the beach glowed in the darkness. My hesitation to take a step forward vanished when the kind stranger followed me. Without fear, I hooked my arm in His. His wisdom would guide me safely home.

"Allison, you are one of the blessed ones. You have a mother that knows how to pray and knows who she serves. God's mercy and grace has been your protection all these years. You will go back home."

"Thank God." The words came forth in a whisper in the still of the night.

"You should be thankful. For some of these young people it's already too late."

"What do you mean?"

"They've gone too far in their rebellion. They love what they are doing, and don't ever want to stop." His words were a little hard to believe at first. I stood in silence.

Breathless words slipped through my fingers that covered my mouth. "I am blessed with a good mother."

"More than you realize, young lady."

"Thank you so much." His loving eyes caressed my heart.

"Thank you for taking time for me." He lifted my chin with the back of his hand.

"You're thanking me?" My surprise thrust itself at Him.

"Yes." He replied. "We need each other." The waves rolled towards us in agreement, breaking softly at our feet.

Adam tilted His head and surveyed the campgrounds with His Spirit. "You had better get back to Meghan. She's looking for you." White sand slid through Adam's fingers, and returned to its place on the beach. He brushed his hands free of the loose particles of sand and started to walk away. "You really do love God." I raced through the thick sand and threw my arms around Him. "Go. Go check on your sister. Oh, and by the way - the name's Adam the Second."

I usually never cried, unless it meant getting people to do what I wanted them to. This time was different from any other.

Grass grew beneath my feet on the narrow path's incline. Within seconds, it was as if the beach had never existed. Thick trees blocked my view, and muffled the sounds of the roaring waters. My mind could not accept my surroundings a forest – so close to a beach.

Meghan let loose an anxious cry for me when she saw me, interspersed with short, choppy breaths. She ran to me as soon as Amaiya let her go.

"I thought I had lost you again."

"No. I'm right here. Things are about to change."

"What do you mean?"

"We are going home."

"You sound sure of that."

"Meghan, I am."

"Allie, I had a dream." Meghan looked past me and into the distance, reliving her dream.

"What about, Megh?"

"It was about a stranger that walked from the beach to my bedside." She pointed in the direction of the thick trees.

"He came from over there."

"What did he look like?"

"He had a kind face and beautiful eyes. The stranger bent down to stroke my hair out of my face. He called me by my name. There were seven other Meghans in our cabin. A couple of them stirred around, but I was the only one awakened by his voice when He called my name."

My own response to the beginning of her dream frightened me. "This place is weird. I hope these things aren't actually happening." Amaiya quieted me down.

"Go on, finish." Amaiya coaxed.

"I leaned on one elbow and looked at Him." She said. "I told him how much I missed Mom. A tear from His eye fell onto my hand. I started to cry after that. I-I cried for a long time. He wanted to know what I was thinking."

Amaiya stroked Meghan's back. "Go on, don't be afraid to say what you need to.

"What did you say to the stranger?"

"I said...I said I miss my daddy." She started to cry again. "Allie, I promise I didn't know I missed him that much. Honest." She pleaded. "Please
don't be mad. I didn't know that my loneliness for him was that big."

"The divorce was a blow to all of us. We were all left wounded." I
replied. Amaiya wiped her eyes and placed her arm around Meghan.

"Is that all of the dream?"

"No." Amaiya answered. "Dreams around here don't end like that."

Meghan took courage to continue. "I told Him I wanted to go home.
He just said, 'Before you leave, Allison will have learned quite a few
valuable lessons'. He was so nice to me, but I yelled at Him."

"It's okay. It was just a dream."

"But I yelled at Him." Amaiya squeezed Meghan's arm, silently
encouraging her to continue the dream. "I told Him that it was not fair
to me and Ian."

He said, "It's not meant to be fair."

I thought we were in trouble because of your bad choices but he
said we weren't. The things we will face on our way home are meant to
bring new direction to our lives. He asked me, "You want peace in your
homes, don't you?" Of course I told him "Yes."

"He sure had a lot to say."

"There's more." Amaiya replied. I motioned with my hand for
Meghan to continue with the rest of the dream. "We talked about
how excited Mom is to see me growing up without giving her major
problems."

"Did he say anything about me?"

"He said He would walk and talk with you along the beachfront."
Meghan pointed to her right. "But I only see trees in front of us. In the
dream, it was a beach with white sand." My mouth dropped open without warning. My eyes failed in finding the path that I had just walked
with the kind stranger.

Amaiya's eyes panned the landscape. "Things are not always what
they seem to be around here."

Meghan's story had left me even more afraid then I had been before. Who was this man? I bowed my head in resolute silence. Would the stranger show up again? Somehow, I felt that Amaiya knew more than she was willing to share.

"Allison, do you think the man in my dream was Jesus?" Meghan had been stewing over that question since having had the dream.

"Don't be silly! It was just a dream." Meghan and Amaiya focused their view on the trees.

"He said he was wisdom for the unwise, and for all who would accept Him. You included."

I had no response for such a statement, but Meghan stood her ground. "I believe Jesus was the wisest man that ever walked planet Earth, Allison. Nobody can change my mind about that."

"You sound just like Mom."

"Is it wrong to sound like my mother?" She buffed her chest out in defense.

"No, no, not when she's right." Meghan was ready for me, if I had given her the least bit of negative resistance against Mom.

I thought the man in Meghan's dream might have been Adam the Second. "Did He by chance give His name?"

"No."

"Try to remember." Meghan backed away. "Did he say Adam?"

"No!"

Amaiya butted in. "You can go see for yourself. Adam lives right over there." She pointed. "He's the garden's groundskeeper."

Hopefully my visit to the groundskeeper would prove to be profitable. I knew I had to visit the groundskeeper, to see if he actually was the Adam I had met (and was possibly also the man from my sister's dream?). These were questions I needed answers to.

"Come on, Megh. Let's go get some rest." We walked back to the cabin, hand in hand. "We have to get up in a couple of hours."

Amaiya frowned. "You seem to have forgotten that you can sleep in as long as you want."

"Oh yeah, that's right."

"Allie, I miss Mom's yelling."

"So do I."

CHAPTER SIX

Nearly Scrambled

Back in our bed, Meghan snuggled as close to me as she possibly could. The kind stranger I met covered us with a blanket. Drifting in and out of sleep prevented me from recognizing the real from a figment of my imagination. I slept peacefully after that whether it was real or not. Peaceful sleep had not been a part of my life since Dad stopped tucking me in at night, when I was in the fourth grade. That's when our parents got divorced, and my nightmares began. I was nine at the time and Meghan was only four.

The next morning I awoke happy and refreshed. Making breakfast for Meghan would make me feel even better. Bacon and eggs with french toast was her favorite breakfast food. She would enjoy breakfast, and I would visit Adam alone to avoid discussions with Him that might otherwise frighten her.

I moved around the kitchen excited about the prospect of smelling bacon frying. I searched in vain for Meghan's favorite breakfast food. Instead the cupboards were filled with sweet snacks of every kind. Amaiya had woken up and followed me around the kitchen.

"Where are the eggs?"

"There are no eggs."

"Bread?"

"Nope."

"Bacon?"

"None. Here, we wake up to colas and chips in the afternoon."

"Well, Meghan's not used to that. She has to have some fruit or something nutritious to eat."

"Good luck." she said. I scraped as much of the icing off a sugary cinnamon bun as I could, and laid it on a napkin next to a bottle of water. "I should be back before she gets out of the shower." She nodded her head in disinterest.

The midmorning breeze pushed me gently toward Adam's small bungalow. It sat nestled between two huge trees. The tiny landscape was beautiful, and the shutters on the house had the same design as the flowers in the flowerbed. Who could imagine Adam living anywhere else?

The fish in the pond stopped swimming to look at me. One of its eyes was half-missing. It wanted to tell me something. I squinted at the bright sun, and looked down at the pond. Without a doubt in my mind, the brightness of the sun caused the illusion with the fish's eyeball. How ridiculous, a fish having one-and-a-half eyeballs.

The smaller of the fish in the pond nudged the strange fish in the side as if to move him along. I hastened from the bridge to get away from the crazy scene.

The doorbell's ringtone calmed me. There was such peace waiting for Adam to answer. He held the door wide open when he saw me. "My home is your home." His smile warmed my heart, and his strong hand squeezed my shoulder. My heart skipped a beat, for I instantly recognized that this was not the touch of the Adam I knew. Furthermore, the Adam I met possessed warmth in his eyes. This man was rough and cold. I took the seat he cordially offered me, and smiled at him.

"You have graced me with your presence, but I must ask why."
"Why?"
"Of course."
"Well," I giggled as I fished for an answer, knowing that an imposter was staring me in the eye.
"Oh Adam, I've heard so much about you. I wanted to see for myself."
"Really?"
"Yes. You take such great care of the grounds around here."
"Well, that is my job, you know." I glanced at the front door. "Would you like some lemonade?"
"No, thank you. It's still a bit early for me."
"All my guests say yes to my lemonade."
"Really Adam, I don't mean any harm. I just don't want any right now."
"You heard what I said, Allison. You can't say no to my lemonade!"

He lifted me off the chair by my arm. "You're hurting me, Adam!" I tried to jerk away, and my ponytail band broke apart. My hair cascaded over my face. I brushed it away from my eyes and waited for his next move. His countenance started to change. "Everything's so confusing around here."

"What is?" I refused to answer. I realized that I may never see Meghan or Ian again. He backed me against the chair.

"Hey, I know you from somewhere...you, you were manning the door at the hotel."

"That's all you need to know."

"Please don't hurt me. I came here for help."

"Why would I help you?" His hands started to close around my throat. I yelled, even though I knew no one would hear me. "Oh God, what have I done? I started to cry." How could I fall apart at a time like this? He was trying to kill me! Finally the lightbulb came on in my head, and I realized that with the Second Adam it is all about faith. I strained to speak. "Help me."

"Shut up!"

Without warning, Adam the Second suddenly appeared between us. He placed His hand on the imposter's neck, and I cringed at the loud cracking noise that followed. The imposter's head tumbled off his shoulders. The false Adam disappeared from sight with his head in his hands.

I rushed into His arms. "Thanks for calling for help." He said.

"The false Adam was trying to kill me!" I paced my breathing, and tried to relax.

"Well, the worst isn't over yet. Evil did not fully manifest itself the way it wanted to. Let's get out of here."

He escorted me across the bridge then lifted his hand without looking behind Him. A stream of prismatic light flew from his index finger into the air. Then, a tiny prismatic lightning bolt dropped straight down on top of its target. The bungalow sank into the ground, and grass, flowers, and trees sprang up in its stead. I stood gazing in wonder.

Adam nodded at the pond. The smaller fish smiled at the larger one. Suddenly, in the blink of an eye the large fish leaped from the pond directly in front of my face. It hung suspended in midair for a few seconds. "He wants you to see his new eye."

"Gosh! Look at that!"

"He tried to warn you not to go inside. He panicked at first, but when he saw me, he knew you'd come out alive." I knelt at the edge of the pond.

"Look, they're gathering around to thank me for my courage."

"How did you know that?"

"When I'm with you, I understand things I normally wouldn't."

"Your sister needs you right now. Don't fear for what you are about to see."

"Why can't we just leave as easily as we came?"

"You have built up a lifetime of rebellions to get to this point. Now, turning things around will take some time." As much as I did not want to hear what He had to say, I knew He was right.

He walked me to the edge of the rolling hill. "Remember - there is more to face on your journey home."

"Thank you, Adam the Second." He watched as I walked away. I took two steps, looked over my shoulder and He was gone.

My hair stood on end at the sudden sound of Meghan's screeching cry. The door to the cabin opened on its own accord just as I reached the porch. The machete Amaiya held in her hands was half her body weight, yet, she was wielding it as if it weighed ounces. Amaiya could have easily severed Meghan's head from her shoulders.

Quietly I asked, "What are you doing?"

The beautiful Hispanic features that had once graced Amaiya's face were now twisted into a mockery of her former beauty. The same fury that had flashed through the false Adam's countenance now surfaced in hers as well. "Back so soon?"

"Amaiya, what's wrong with you!?" She came at me with the machete. I flung the door open in front of her. The blade slashed into the door panel, ripping it half off its hinges.

"Meghan, run!"

Using the door, I pinned Amaiya against the wall. She swung again, and the machete missed my torso by inches. Suddenly, I was aware of the Second Adam's presence, though I did not see Him. A ray of light shot out from the hole in Adam's right wrist and held the door steady.

"Amaiya, what happened to you?" The words pushed through the emotion I felt. "How could you do this to us? We trusted you!" My chest heaved with disappointment.

"I'm stuck here forever"

"That's not true. It's all in what you believe."

"I hate you Allison!" Amaiya started inching out from behind the door.

"Here, let me help you. I insisted." I moved the door, putting Amaiya in the perfect position for a powerful headbutt. The strike put her flat on her back, and I ran without looking back.

I caught up with Meghan on the front yard to find ourselves surrounded by dozens of creatures. They were obviously the teenagers we had met before. Their zombie-like appearance made my hair stand on end.

"There are so many of them. What are we going to do?"

"Whatever you do, don't let go of my hand, Megh. Hold your arm up to shield them from you."

"The man in the dream said to sing in the midst of harm and danger."

"What?"

"How long will an arm shield protect us anyway?"

"I guess it's worth a shot. Do it!"

Meghan sang "He Reigns Forever," with graceful poise. An air of peace covered that section of the garden, and threw the creatures in disarray. In confusion, they fled to the other side of the garden, and hid there until the next evening.

We found out later that the Ghoulians fluctuated from the entrance of the garden, where the rotten fruit was to the outskirts of Choco Valley. They did whatever they could as an excuse to habitate on Choco territory.

CHAPTER SEVEN

Narrow Escape

I awakened that morning with my mind set on escaping the garden. I could not think of anything else. The unavailability of fruit was making me paranoid, and candy and chips had lost their appeal. I was tired of loud music, and of boys calling me their 'thang'. In my paranoia, Meghan never visited the restroom alone. I was too afraid of losing her again.

Ian's absence had suddenly hit me like a ton of bricks, and we began searching for him every day. I am not sure how far our legs had carried us as we searched the garden. Or for that matter, how long it had been since we had eaten a good meal. Yesterday's search for Ian landed us back in front of the garden entrance near the Ghoulians' habitat. Although we saw no Ghoulians, we ran for our lives. We felt blessed and cursed at the same time to have made it this far.

Furthermore, I had come to my wit's end, and could do nothing more to cheer Meghan. She walked with her eyes focused on the ground.

"The tiny tree lined path." I whispered. "Amaiya!" My voice escalated.

"Where?" Meghan yelled, ready to run. We heard the commotion from the cola ponds in the distance.

"She said to remember the shortcut. That it would come in handy."

"I know she's gone, but I don't trust her shortcut."

"It's too late for that, Megh. We walked that trail about twenty-five minutes ago." Meghan felt more at ease and slowed down her pace.

"Look, Megh." The compass on my key ring pointed west. I pointed to the billboard sign. My little sister hunched her shoulders, and read the billboard. "Welcome to West Morganstone." The moment she spoke, it felt like home. It smelled like home, too. The fragrance of flowers was everywhere, and Meghan's arms were filled with the flowers before I could tell her to stop. We had been through so much together. I would welcome anything that made her happy for a change.

Emily's Commissary was the first store we had come in contact with since our arrival to the garden. It was about forty yards from the entrance billboard. Her store was massive – just name the item, and she had supply of it.

One section of the store displayed vases of every kind. Meghan loved the metallic vases more than the glass, ceramic, and mirrored ones. In the next section, baskets of all shapes, colors and sizes adorned the next six aisles. They covered the wall to my left, and hung from the ceiling as well.

The store owner was Emily herself, and she had come to the garden at the age of nineteen. She greeted us and gave us a key to our new home. We were told she would take good care of us, as long as we resided on the west side of the garden. It was true - Emily *was* good to us. We wanted for nothing. Nor did we have to go elsewhere for anything, unless we wanted to.

Our home was located in a gated community. The streets were lined with trees and driveways, and there was a park across the way. It reminded us of our Michigan subdivision – lacking only Mom's presence, and Dad's occasional drive-by visits. This had been the happiest two weeks of our lives as residents of West Morganstone.

We loved everything about our new surroundings. The many talented young people there with us never produced a dull moment. The calendar of events was renewed every ten years so that everyone had an opportunity at the events they wanted to participate in. Weekly musical concerts, and every sport imaginable were easy to find. There were always plenty of actors and actresses available and on call when needed. Yet there was something missing at every event. No one dared to speak about the empty space that occupied the stands at each event.

In retrospect, I remembered the way things used to be when my three-year-old sister had performed as a flower in the spring performance of *Gardens and Belles*. Mom had clapped her hands until they were aching and whistled louder than Dad, with her fingers between her teeth. Meghan's round face had been the perfect center for the daisy she performed as. Nothing, absolutely nothing, could take the place of having parents around to attend our activities.

I came back to my senses just as the west-siders finished a perfect tennis match against the east side. Meghan laid her hand on top of mine. She smiled a sad smile, and gathered her things to leave. Ian had always loved tennis - her thoughts must have been with him.

We expected the search team later today, and they would continue the search for Ian. Fifty people from the other side of the island had volunteered to organize small search parties, and were combing the area. We hoped they would find him before nightfall. This was the fifth day of the search for Ian on this side of the garden.

Back at our new house, Meghan handed me a tiny plant. "Allison, could you live here without Mom?" I stuck the last flower in the hole in the ground, and gave it a pat or two to secure it in place. I quickly scanned my brain for the right answer.

"I've been asking myself that same question."

"Do you feel almost satisfied with her not being around?"

"It's a strange feeling, but I can almost say yes. Way down deep I still miss her though." I quickly changed the subject. "Here. You water our new babies while I wash up. I'm making Mom's homemade soup for dinner tonight."

"Yay! Let's go to the market." She said and leaped slightly off the ground.

At the market, Emily had everything set aside we needed for Mom's homemade soup. Swiss cheese and flax seed bread was one of Mom's favorite grilled sandwiches for soup and both ingredients were already in the bag. Sometimes, Emily knew things without having ever been told. This made me extremely suspicious of her.

"How's it going, girls?"

"We just finished our flower bed this afternoon." Meghan reported.

"I would love to see it sometime." Emily's blonde hair enthusiastically bounced off her shoulders and cascaded down her back.

"Emily, Megh and I would like to thank you for everything you've done for us."

"That's why I'm here. We are here to serve."

"This is the first sound sleep we've had since Ian's been missing." Meghan explained.

"Hopefully something will turn up from today's search." Emily replied.

"They've been out there for five days now." I concluded.

Meghan and I observed and enjoyed Emily's hospitality towards us. In return, our expressions of gratitude were menial. "Emily, how would you like to come over for soup and sandwiches?"

Meghan rocked back and forth from heel to toe. "Yeah, you can see the flower bed then, and enjoy my piano playing as a bonus." She grinned.

"That sounds lovely." Emily's soft chuckles flowed melodiously.

Upon return from the market, one of the search parties sent out to find Ian hailed us. "Good news." Ethan proclaimed. He removed his glasses.

"You found Ian?" Meghan asked.

"I didn't say that." Ethan remarked. Jordan came closer to me and spoke directly to me. "We know where he can be found."

"What's the difference?" Meghan asked with a question mark expression written on her face.

"I mean we know where to look. But we still have to search for him. Make sense?"

"Now it does."

Ethan stood in rank next to Jordan and re-adjusted his glasses as he spoke. "We found a couple of things that might help us figure out where he's gone."

I identified them right away, and reached for the items. "He never goes anywhere without his hair comb and pocket knife." I said. Jordan pointed at the torn blue jean fabric lying in the palm of Ethan's hand. "Someone found it stuck to a fence post on the other side of the island."

"There's chocolate on it." Jordan emphasized with his hands.

I sniffed the material and nodded. Jordan concluded by saying, "It looks like he may have tried to jump the fence. Probably to escape the Ghoulians that hide along the outskirts of Choco Valley."

Meghan took a closer look at Ethan's face. "Hey, you're wearing my cousin's glasses! He doesn't see very well without them." I tried comforting Meghan to keep her from breaking down in front of everyone.

Jordan took the glasses off Ethan's face and handed them to my little sister. Then, he said to the search team, "Let's go. We'll let you know what's going on before the night is over."

I thanked Jordan and Ethan with a frail smile. Meghan examined the torn blue jean fabric and covered it with her fist. She wiped her eyes a second time. The search party walked through the wooded area to cross back over the river.

Unexpectedly Emily poked her head over my shoulder, and gently nudged me with the salad bowl.

"I made a salad for dinner."

"Thank you, Emily."

"Are you ready for your musical performance, Meghan?" Meghan hugged me, and we walked back to the house arm-in-arm. Emily was annoyed by my sister's silence, and tried to start a conversation.

"Meghan, what color dress are you wearing for this evening's performance?" Meghan remained silent, and I pinched her hard underneath her forearm. She flinched.

"Now Allison," Emily's voice deepened, "that was not necessary. She didn't deserve a pinch that hard."

"Meghan knows better than to be rude."

"I'm sorry, Emily." She apologized. "Really, I am. I miss Ian a lot."

Emily's need to control things exploded across the board. She had completely changed our dinner menu by the time we arrived home. Now Meghan was excited about dinner and her performance. She rushed upstairs to take a bath before dinner. In the meantime, Emily and I decided to get better acquainted.

"What is it that you are looking for here in West Morganstone?" I babbled for an answer. "Well frankly, I can't answer that yet. I've hardly been a resident of the community for two weeks. I love it here." My smile quickly faded from my face.

"Frankly," she responded, "I think Meghan will do just fine here as a permanent resident. Her people skills are strong for a young girl her age."

I saw through Emily's scheme to persuade my sister to stay in Morganstone if Ian and I decided to leave. I was certain of it as she continued. "Oh yes, I think she should stay...and I think she'll want to stay. I'm sure you agree."

I was beginning to have serious doubts about Emily and her kindnesses, and I am certain she picked upon it. The residents of the garden made me paranoid about everything especially after Amaiya's betrayal. From that moment on, I knew I had to devise a plan of escape from West Morganstone.

The smell of dinner rolls lured Meghan to the table. The food was delicious, and we were all too busy eating to engage in small talk. I noticed that Meghan did not say grace before dinner, which was unusual for her. In fact, this was the very first time that I could think of that she had ever done that. Mom had always seen to it that she never forgot.

I watched Emily watch Meghan in delight as she gobbled down her food.

"All right," I softly demanded, "it's time to serenade us." She burped several times, and tripped over the table leg on her way to the piano. "Be careful!" My voice echoed in the room. Emily's stomach ached from laughter, and Meghan laughed just as hard.

My sister switched from giddy excitement to refined concentration within a matter of seconds. Her fingers stroked the keys with such beautiful precision. As she played, Emily's body swayed in time to the music. She closed her eyes and clutched her right hand over her fist.

After the performance Emily hugged her. "It, it was magnificent. And the color of your dress perfectly suited the style of music."

"Don't you just love the color red, Emily?"

"Yes, I do. It was worth coming over here this evening." I stared at Meghan's purple dress and wondered what was going on.

Emily walked to the staircase railing. "Excuse me ladies, I must freshen up." Meghan did not say much while Emily was upstairs.

"What color is your dress?"
"Red." She replied.
"Are you okay? Look at me." She would not. By that time Emily had re-entered the room.

"Emily, when do you think the boys will return?"
"Who knows? They are probably somewhere playing a game of touch football."
"Well, you know boys will be boys."

She clapped her hands together, and revved up her arms in front of her. "Why don't we go for a walk? Maybe we'll see them on the way." I finished clearing the dinner table and at Emily's suggestion, we prepared ourselves for a walk.

Meghan volunteered to change into her red jeans and t-shirt. "When you change clothes Allie, dress like me." "Whatever makes you happy, little sis.

Meghan bounced down the stairs dressed in purple jeans. She glanced at me, but never gave me a straightforward look. Again, Emily complimented her. I changed my clothes in imitation of Meghan, and Emily raved about my appearance as well. Meghan got a kick out of Emily's reactions.

On our way out the door Emily volunteered to stop by the store to pick up a few flashlights, some rope, and duct tape in case we needed them. "What do you have in mind for these items, Emily?"
"Well, you never know what you may run into, when you're searching for someone who's lost."
"That is so kind of you." I replied, but Meghan remained silent.

"I'm almost certain I know where he is."
"Where do you suggest we look?"
"Just follow me."
"Gladly."

The moon was shining brightly that night, so we attached the flashlights to our hiking belts to begin our uphill climb. I extended my hand to Meghan for leverage. I smelled dinner rolls after I lifted her up over the ridge. Meghan put her finger to her lips to shush me and turned away. I was sure the dinner rolls were for Ian...so what was the big secret? Nothing made sense anymore. Meghan had not looked me in the eye since yesterday. I realized that is when she had become friendlier with Emily.

Emily motioned for us to sit among the rocks, explaining that it would be hard for anyone to spot us. Jordan and his search team had no idea that Emily had been trailing them. Who could not help but see us as bright as the moonlight was? Even hiding in the rocks was not going to make much difference. Of course, rather than put up a fuss and make things worse, I held my tongue. I had no clue of what Emily might be capable of doing. Even my sister was quick to do whatever Emily asked her to.

In three minutes flat, my sister was asleep, and I was well on the way. After some time, Emily gently shook my shoulder. "Allison. Allison, we have to go." I gently removed Meghan's head from my shoulder, and we fell in line behind Emily to continue our journey. Emily said that the path would lead us eastward.

"Hey Megh, the moon is softening now. It's not as bright as it was when we started our journey." She would not speak to me, but shook her head in disagreement with what I had just spoken. For once, I could not figure out what was going on with my sister.

"Look!" Emily exclaimed. "There's Jordan and Ethan."

Meghan gave the cabin her undivided attention. "I bet anything that Ian's in that cabin." The guys were gambling outside the cabin, with cigarettes and wine coolers by their sides. Three campfires were burning brightly and lounge chairs with blankets were among them.

"You two wait here until I come back to get you." Emily strutted toward the campsite with authority. She demanded they let Ian go.

Ethan replied. "How much longer are you going to pretend that you're their friend, Emily? Do they know that this was part of our plan?"

She motioned for him to lower his voice. "Don't start with me, Ethan. My friends are over there beyond those trees. Give us Ian and we will leave."

As they were talking Meghan pulled two red ski masks from her hiking pouch. "Here. Put this on. Don't ask any questions." She pointed to the moon. "Allie, look at the moon."

"What in the-? There's no such thing as the man in the moon!"

"It's not just a man. It's a silhouette of Adam the Second."

"What!" I gasped.

"He's in front of the moon." I put the ski mask on as quickly as I could. "Follow my lead, and don't say a word." She ordered. This time Meghan did not have to tell me twice.

"Allison. Come quick." Meghan put the glasses on and faced me. "Do whatever you see me do. You got that?"

"I got it." Meghan walked fearlessly through the camp in plain view of everyone. She came up to one of the four boys that were drinking wine coolers. Meghan snatched the wine cooler from him and poured it out on the ground, and then threw the empty bottle to me. I tossed it into the bushes. Cameron's eyes followed the bottle, but his eyes glided past us as though we were not even there. "Did you see that?"

"Hey dude, I saw it man." Samuel rubbed his eyes in disbelief.

Meghan called out. "You're simply too young to drink."

"Who said that?...Where are you?" The boys looked around for the source of the voice, causing a ruckus in the camp.

"You're too young to drink!" I exclaimed.

"It's her!" Cameron followed my voice to the trees where the hammocks were.

"Who?" Samuel asked.

"Kim Li, my ex."

"What?" Samuel weaved a little from side to side. "John Li, did you hear that?" His voiced carried across the campsite. John Li swaggered to the campfire in the middle of the camp grounds.

John Li greeted everyone in a soothing baritone voice. "Man, Cameron says your sister is here. He's looking for her now."

John Li wasted no time in defending his sister. "That's not possible. She rebelled against the garden. She stayed behind with our Mom."

Samuel turned his head to point at Cameron, whose head was in the bushes as he searched for Kim Li.

"Kim Li, come on out, baby! I know you're here!"

"She's not here I tell you!" John Li took a few steps forward with his fists clenched, with Cameron still facing the bushes.

"Well, who's doing these things, then? She still wants me!" John Li reached for Cameron, and Cameron let out a defensive squeal.

Meghan set a branch on fire and threw it across the campsite. A couple of blankets draped across the lounge chairs went up in flames. The flames from the fire quickly spread across the campgrounds. As the fire spread, a fist fight broke out between Cameron and John Li. They fought while Sam and the others put out the fire.

That's when we made our way over to a guy puffing on a cigarette, a little farther away. I jerked the pack of cigarettes out of his hand, and threw it into the campfire. Then I pushed another guy into him and another brawl broke out. By the time we finished instigating fights, the trailer door opened and out walked Ian. He had a girl on each arm, and two more following him. I spoke to him, but he paid no attention to me. He was determined to stay put.

"Megh, did you hear that? Someone just called you." It was the Second Adam. He and Ian were hiding beside a tree. But...Ian was still in the middle of the camp. So which one was real? If that really was Adam the Second, why would He be hiding? He had been a champion at the bungalow.

In the midst of the confusion in the camp, I too, was wracked with confusion. I did not know what to do. "Ian, let's go. We came to get you." I said, to the Ian in the middle of the camp.

I saw Adam the Second put his hand over the other Ian's mouth. I called for Ian a second time. Both Ians looked in the direction of my voice. The one in the camp could not see me, but it looked like he was trying to figure out where I was. Meghan tried to get me to hush, but I had reached my breaking point.

"For the last time, Ian, let's go! I'm not leaving without you!" I ripped the mask off my face, and everyone in the camp looked at me.

"There she is. Get her!" Ethan and Jordan, the search team captains raised their hands to the sky. The twelve guys, Emily, and the Ian in the camp turned into some kind of water creatures. They had the face of a tortoise, the body and tail of a scorpion, and strange fin-like wings though capable of walking on two legs. The thick scales that covered their bodies allowed them to breathe on land. They rushed after me, and I knew that this was the end of life as I knew it.

Meghan caught up with me as I was running. "Put your hood back on! The color red is invisible to them!" I opened the hood to cover my face, but in my haste, I dropped it between my legs. She pulled her own mask off and scooped mine up, telling me to keep running.

"Now, do what I do." We managed to trip up a few of the creatures by dodging in and out from among the trees. Racing through the forest brought us to a sudden dead end. There was no place to go except over a cliff.

"Now what? And please don't say jump!"

"On the count of three, pull your mask down over your face and fall flat on the ground." We flung ourselves onto the ground, and the water creatures plunged over the side of the cliff. The crushing of bones and animal cries rang out. Meghan crawled to me on her hands and knees. "Are you all right?"

I looked into her eyes and screamed uncontrollably. Her pupils were red. They had gotten to her. That's why her attitude was so different at the house. I should have seen it coming. She and Emily fit like a hand in a glove.

"Look at me!" She yelled. "I'm okay." Her eyes slowly faded back to their natural color. "Adam the Second did this to me when the search party went into the woods."

"Why?"

"He needed Emily to welcome me fully as a resident of the garden."

"Is that why you wouldn't look at me when I asked you to?"

"Think about it. You would have really freaked out if you had seen me like this at home." I pulled her close and she held on. "What about Ian?" "There's nothing to worry about. He's with Adam the Second. So, I calmed down and enjoyed one of the dinner rolls Meghan had packed.

CHAPTER EIGHT

The Crossover

After that incident, I did not know where to take Meghan for her safety. I trusted absolutely no one in the garden.

The stretch of meadow before us was picturesque and pleasant to pass through. After reaching the bottom of the rolling meadow, we found another slope to climb. Climbing it put us at the brink of a river. The river's edge guided us through the valley, comforting us with its calmness.

Numerous twists and turns in the riverbed made it dangerous to cross over on foot. Finally, the river's course straightened out a bit. Shallow places were far and in between. When we happened upon the shallowest part of the river, I thought it made sense to cross it.

Meghan suggested that we ask God what to do. I told her I already had the answer. "Okay, Miss Wisdom." She said and bowed her head. "Lord, I have not spoken to you since Amaiya turned into a monster and tried to kill me. Please get us out of this mess that Allison got us into. Thanks again, my man of great wisdom. Amen." She laughed to herself, and I pretended not to hear.

"Look!" Meghan demanded. "Over there!" She stood motionless and let go of my hand.

"It's a pair of black framed glasses." I forgot all about my brooding when I realized the glasses belonged to Ian.

"Ian!" My sister yelled with her hands cupped to the sides of her mouth. "Ian, where are you?"

"Not so loud." He groaned. Ian was lying on the ground on the other side of the tree farthest away from the river.

"Boy, am I glad to see you." Meghan rushed his glasses over to him.

"I'm glad to see you, too."

"Ian, are you all right?"

"I'm just shaken up a bit. I don't know exactly how I ended up here." He stood to his feet and straightened his clothes, and we vowed to remain inseparable from that point on.

"I will be a changed person by the time I get home." Ian remarked. Meghan nodded in agreement. Suddenly, a deep silence settled all around us. The birds stopped tweeting. The squirrels buried their heads in their paws. Friendly animal play ceased, and the fawns hid among the trees. We looked for the source of the silence we were feeling - it was obvious that it was alive. "Stop it!" Meghan demanded. "Stop pushing me!" She swung at thin air.

The strange force lifted Ian into the air feet first. "Whoa!" He cried. He hung suspended, scared out of his wits. My sister bumped into Ian as she was lifted up, and bounced off him. On cue, my arms flew above my head and I was spinning like a top as I was lifted high into the air. Whatever had taken ahold of us then flew us back towards the ground, low enough to see the fish in the clear river water below us.

I was afraid for my little sister as we traveled over the river. The invisible force held her by the front of her shirt. Her arms and legs dangled. Would the force drop her in the middle of the river? I was ready to bargain with it for whatever it was worth. Flashes of light pulsed over her. In an instant, the claws that gripped her shirt materialized and became visible. Then scaley legs and feathers appeared. On the third flash of light, several gruesome vultures fully materialized. They were more than hideous, and obviously did not belong on that side of the valley. Meghan screamed for two solid minutes and fainted dead away.

The vultures had two sets of spindly fangs at the corners of their mouths that curled at the ends, and their breath was horrible.

"Hey Pete?"

"Yeah, Max?"

"Do you think this bunch can be persuaded to cross over?"

"Don't know. Let's see what Shifty has to say."

"Hey, try to wake the little one up."

"Okay Pete."

"Where are you taking us?" Ian asked. The bird that held onto Ian stayed focused on his flying as he spoke. "You are going to the low end."

"You mean the south side of the garden? Please say no." I begged. "We've heard horror stories about the south side." They just laughed. Meghan came to, and smelled the vultures' breath, and fainted again.

Our captors swooped low to cruise over the top of the garbage heap that contained body parts. The stench from below was truly vile this close, and I felt slugs crawling up my legs. My screams bounced off the mountaintops as I thrashed about, trying to get rid of the slugs. The smell of decay and corruption were nauseating. Ian vomited several times as we flew.

"Hey Pete," "Yeah Max," Pete responded.

"Let's help Missy out. Bring her over here."

"My pleasure Pete." Holding me by the nape of my collar, Pete swung me from side to side with Max on one side and the oldest vulture of the three on the other. Max plucked a slug off my pant leg. "The first one goes to you, Pete." He slung it high and dropped it into Pete's beak.

"Thanks Max."

"Think nothing of it, Petie." The old vulture smiled at me, and caught three slugs at once and swallowed them whole. They raved over Salami's skill, which had apparently taken him many years to master.

Pete hollered with glee. "Not many can do that without choking!" Their laughter ran chills up and down my spine.

Salami spoke cunningly to Ian. His whisper released vapors that influenced Ian's mind. Salami's voice was deep and rich, sweet and stern. In seconds, Ian developed a positive impression of Sal. After that, his stomach settled down. He took a deep breath, and enjoyed our flight. I frowned in thought.

We arrived at the south side of the garden in time to see two groups preparing for battle. The vultures told us that the nerdiacs and machoramas were going to fight, and predicted that this would be the most vicious war ever fought between the two. The bloodiest warrior would be declared the victor, and would be regarded as one of the highest officials in the entire garden.

The vultures flew even lower over the weaponry unit. The unit's machinery was designed to sever arms, legs and heads from bodies. Hacksaws, knives, broken bottles and baseball bats were piled high. Tables were set up with intravenous needles and bags for lethal injections that would leave the bravest victim screaming for mercy. These measures would ensure a slow, painful death.

Meghan had not stopped crying since we landed on the ground. The crowd that surrounded us included some of the Ghoulians from Choco Valley. They were not as scary here as they had been on the other side of the valley.

Salami, Max and Pete surrounded us, and forced us to walk down into the valley. We were on our way to meet Shifty, the King of Rebellion

Dungeon. He would make the final decision of our fate, if we did not comply to crossing over to the southside way of life.

By now, Ian had crossed over fully to the other side against his cousins. Salami watched him with deep satisfaction.

We stopped in front of a giant marquee that read 'Rebellion's Dungeon'. Flames of fire shot from the marquee. The welcoming committee in front of us rapped to us about the downside of being there without joining a gang. They hummed for rhythm, kept time with garbage can lids, and created a melody by blowing into bottles. The rest of them danced to the music, and Ian was right in there with them. Ian's eyebrows now arched up his forehead just like Salami's, and his face grew more distorted the more he danced. My cousin smelled like the others, and felt right at home in the atmosphere.

"Join us, join us, join us." They shouted. Flames from the sign reached for us. Meghan and I backed away as far as we could.

"Come on, cousins." Ian coaxed. "You don't know what you're missing." His smooth tone of voice resonated with Meghan. She began tapping her foot along with the music.

I shuffled my little sister behind me. "Meghan, don't listen to him. Ian, come to your senses. This is not the place you want to be. Remember home. Remember Aunt Jennifer."

Ian's behavior suddenly brought to mind one of the few short stories I did remember from bedtime long ago. Ian was reminding me of the story of the prodigal son – he was behaving like a modern-day prodigal son from Farmington Hills, Michigan. In the New Testament, the prodigal son went wild after he left home. He lived carelessly, and threw his inheritance away on a partying lifestyle. He found himself broke, and without a place to stay after his spending spree. The only job he could find was tending hogs. He had smelled like a hog, and ate whatever they ate.

The prodigal son made new friends easily because of his money. His new friends were scandalous and lustful, and he had become one of them. When he ran out of money, they ran out on him. That's when he realized his big mistake. He was not prepared to take on the world. He had left home too soon.

Fortunately, the story had a happy ending. The son humbled himself and went back to his rich father. He asked for forgiveness, and the father received his son back from his spiritual death.

I knew that somehow the Heavenly Father would find an opening in Ian's heart. Ian had crossed over and had become a prodigal. He had become extremely generous and wasteful with his personality, with his soul. We watched him devour vulture droppings with Salami. We tried to get him to stop, but it was impossible to distract Ian away from the vultures.

Abruptly, Ian ran over to one of the nearby hacksaw devices. Ian summoned help and four Ghoulians picked me up and laid me on the table. "Ian, how could you do this?" He ignored me, and connected my arms and legs to the hacksaw device. My sister danced around the table in glee,
singing their dreadful song. I screamed in fear. "Help me, Meghan! Please! Don't do this! Think about what you're doing!" Then I blacked out.

I woke up and found my clothes soaked with perspiration. Even the ground around me was wet. Ian was shaking me so hard his nails dug into my flesh.

"Allie, wake up. It's okay. It was just a dream. We're safe now."

Meghan awakened crying. "I was there too. I couldn't stop dancing. I'm sorry, Allie."

"I couldn't stop laughing." Ian commented.

"I don't remember falling asleep." I shook my head, as if shaking myself back to my senses.

"Me neither. It's weird." Meghan yelped.

"Are you two hungry?" He asked.

"No." We answered in unison.

"Let's get out of here." I responded.

A black and white bird sat on a low tree branch watching us. His legs were crossed and it made me wonder what it was up to. Meghan inched her way to the tree trunk. I tried stopping her. "It may be a Ghoulian. It could be Emily."

"Don't be silly." She said. "His smile is different." Its beautiful tail swept across her face as he turned to perch on her shoulder. Meghan nodded toward the direction we should take. "Now, let's go." she said. The bird flew to me and perched on my shoulder.

We talked about our strange dream until we came to a fork in the road. The path to the right was lined with houses that spiraled down into a ravine. The houses sat close together, and wild animals had invaded the foreboding community. Dark clouds hung low overhead. Animals howled, and the wind stirred up the river that looked like it could overflow its banks at any time. I eyed the river bank's course down one side of the ravine and up the other. Its final resting place was in front of a huge mansion that sat on a hill.

To our left, the sky was as clear as could be. The trees on the left side of the fork in the road were healthy and loaded with fruit. There were houses in neat rows that formed a small town. The mansion looked like a toy dollhouse from where we stood. Of course, I knew instantly which road we should take.

Ian spoke up before I could persuade him otherwise. "The less desirable path would be more profitable." He announced. I refused to listen. I pointed in the direction of the clear sky and tiny town. He and Meghan started down the right lane without hesitation.

I refused to follow. My way made more sense. After all, the sky over the left path was bright and sunny. Daylight would help us make better time. Ian was wrong this time. There was nothing to second guess about.

Still, my dear cousin continued to fight. "Think it over before you follow that path." Apparently Ian was no longer threatened by my presence. "We won't let you do this to us again." Ian took steps to block my way. "You see things the way they seem, not the way they really are." "I disagree with you this time." I protested.

"Just like all of the time, Allison." My sister retorted.

Ian tried one last time to convince me otherwise. "Allie, have you forgotten that the Garden of Youth is no longer on your side? Once you decide to leave the garden, it fights back." They walked toward the dark path, and stopped to give me one last chance to change my mind.

The beautiful black and white bird still perched on my shoulder, snatched the bag of candy from Meghan's hand. He tossed it onto the left path just as I attempted to set my foot down on the pavement. A steel gate slammed shut, sealing the opening completely off. "That could have been us!" Meghan gasped.

"At least we know what's on that side of the steel gate." Ian added. Ferocious dogs the size of horses leaped high enough for us to see what we had missed. Their fangs were so enormous, they nearly touched the ground.

Ian and Meghan thanked God for His guidance, and humbly started down the path on the right towards the mansion. I followed, shame and embarrassment taunting me all the way.

CHAPTER NINE

Forever Present

It was only noon, yet my doubts about making it to the mansion before dark overpowered me. After all, we were on foot. Questions tumbled through the channels of my mind, gripping me with fear. I had gotten us into this, but I could not get us out. What if we never got home? What if we did not make it out alive? And the Second Adam...with my head in my hands, I complained about His absence. My heart knew that the Second Adam wanted to help, but would He come through this time? I sat down under a tree defeated, and tossed twigs into the river, paralyzed by my thoughts.

"What's wrong with you?" Ian grabbed my arm to pull me up. The strength I felt in his hand was supernatural. I jerked away from him and straightened my clothes. "It's not like you to give up and bury your head in the sand. We have a journey to make, and we have to do it before nightfall." Meghan stomped her foot. "I agree!" I just sat back down and folded my arms.

At a moment's glance, the mansion on the hill caught my eye. I stood to my feet, and stepped closer in full view of the mansion. "Do you see what I see?"

"What?" Ian and Meghan asked at the same time.

"Someone's standing on the walkway of the mansion."

"That's ridiculous," Meghan tooted her lips out, "You can't see that far." She turned her back to the mansion.

"It's Him. It's really Him!"

"Who, the Second Adam?" Ian asked.

"You know the Second Adam?"

"I met Him the night I was all alone. He reassured me that you would find me today."

"Really?"

Meghan folded her arms. "I don't know what to make of this."

"Look!" Ian cried out. "He's waving at us." Ian and I waved back.

Meghan looked toward the hill. "Oh my God!" she gasped. "It's the man from my dream!" She ran as fast as she could, and we joined her. Filled with excitement, I played tag with my sister along the way. We picked flowers as we ran. Ian joined in and played leapfrog. Excitement mounted the closer we got to the foot of the hill. Immediately my legs grew heavy. Ian and Meghan slowed down to a standstill.

"Do you hear that?" I asked.

"Don't start!" Ian shouted.

"There it is again."

Heads popped up all around us. Short and tall creatures came at us from all directions. The tallest one pounced on Ian, and knocked him to the ground. A playful childlike creature pulled Meghan's hair and stepped on her foot. She cried for Mommy and the Second Adam. I fought the creatures single handedly. Ian and Meghan broke away from the creatures and ran to the mansion, and I followed.

We sat on the grassy knoll in front of the mansion to catch our breath. A spokesperson for the Second Adam scurried to us, quickly reassuring us that the creatures were harmless. With a stroke or two of Meghan's hair, the old man successfully calmed her down. He waited for the chattering crew to catch up with us.

"Come with me. We shouldn't leave Master Adam waiting." The man said to us.

"John, I AM here. I will take them in."

"Yes sir."

"Make sure the woodles get fed and bedded down for the evening."

"Yes sir. I will check in before you retire for the night, sire."

"Thanks, John." John executed a bow to Adam the Second and lovingly showed the woodles their sleeping quarters for the evening. "Oh and John, prepare the woodles for our next guests. Expect them a couple of days from now."

"Yes sire. It will take that long to prepare them anyhow." John bowed and the creatures waved good bye to us.

"Stop staring and get up." The Second Adam kindly ordered. "The woodles were unleashed to get you here faster. I would never do anything to harm you. They are playful creatures."

At that, Meghan waved me aside and took Adam the Second by the hand. "I'm hungry."

"Right this way."

The table He directed us to was the most lavish table we had ever seen. It was approximately twenty-four feet long. Every vegetable and fruit imaginable was available, and it made up for all the times we had none. The Second Adam was kind. We ate our fill, and He said we could take as much as we could at the time of our departure.

The next morning, we rose very early. After breakfast, the Second Adam gave us vague details of how we would endure more challenging situations. However, He never spoke about what we would face head-on. I was used to being in control of things, and wanted to know how much control He had of the outcome of our trials. Although He promised to never leave us without hope, help, or heaven's best, I still had questions.

The Second Adam's way of thinking did not always make sense to me. For instance, He said that our departure from Him did not mean we would be ending our discourse with Him. Without a hope of understanding what He meant, to avoid looking stupid, I kept my mouth shut. Meghan, on the other hand, looked deeply into Adam the Second's eyes and asked, "What does that mean?"

"Just because you're returning home doesn't mean you don't want to hear My voice or desire My wisdom anymore."

Meghan looked in my direction. "Did you hear that, Allison?" I sampled my rice apricot dish and pretended my sister was not in the room. She sat closest to the Second Adam, and clung to His every word. It put Ian and me to shame. We both became more attentive after we noticed the way she was behaving.

"Hey," she pushed her chair from under her and stood in front of Him, "You are the man in my dream. You are the one." She lifted His right hand to her cheek and kissed the nail scar in His wrist. "I love you." She sat on His lap and placed His arms securely around her and closed her eyes.

My sister's discovery shocked me and my cousin. I fell to my knees next to Ian asking the Second Adam to forgive me. My self-centeredness had prevented me from seeing who He really was.

"It is true. You must come to trust me as a little child." He embraced us, and wiped away our tears. My life was changed never to doubt Him as God again. "Just remember, I Am always there for you." Making my peace with God kept me there until the next morning.

CHAPTER TEN

Breakthrough

After we bundled up, the Second Adam walked us to the edge of the hill. "Your destination is before you." Meghan's voice echoed from among the trees. "I know, I know. Don't look back."

"Keep them in line!"

"Don't worry, I've got this!" Meghan responded.

Our journey led us beneath the surface of the earth. We walked the spiraled path. For safety's sake, we stopped walking until our eyes adjusted to the dark. Meghan held on to Ian's waist, and I held on to her shoulders. Loose rock crumbled beneath Ian's feet and splashed in the water beneath us. We clung to each other, and waited for Meghan to calm down. It took a while before we could convince her to take another step.

Finally the trail ended at the mouth of a cave. The hole in the rock was less inviting than the darkness we had just passed through. We prepared our minds to crawl inside that hole in the ground.

We stared at the site, unwilling to go any further. Glowing embers of light suddenly appeared and covered us, warming us from the inside out. Ian indicated that he was ready to enter the cave, and Meghan agreed. To my own surprise, my first step initiated us into the blackness. They followed.

The cave's threshold met us with waves of bitter cold. Dampness radiated from the walls of the cave and soaked my face; coldness nibbled at my fingers and toes. Once inside, the sparkles of light surrounding us vanished as quickly as they had appeared.

My pockets bulged with the mittens that John had stuffed inside them. In frustration, he had forced a fleecy lamb poncho into my arms. The deeper we traveled in the cave the colder it became. Boy, was I glad that I had eventually listened to John.

To pass the time, Ian recited the Discourse of the Good Shepherd from the early 1600's, and Meghan sang the twenty-third Psalm. Even in the darkness, time past more quickly while they sang or spoke.

At Ian's advice, we followed the sound of dripping water. The drips were so faint; we had to stand still to distinguish their direction. We could not take a chance on following the wrong path.

The drips grew louder, and our path widened. I began to feel better about our chances of survival. Meghan pointed at the ceiling of the cave. The light that slipped through the cracks made it possible for us to clearly exit the cave.

The walls of the cave bore many names, evidence of those who had survived the journey to this point. Meghan, of course, read as many names as she could. "Rachel Z., Olivia, Marcus, Bernie, Wynona, Janet O., Victor F., wow, look at all these names, George, Frank, and Richard."

"I see the names, Megh. I just want to get out of here and forget what we've just come through." Ian fired up like a hot air balloon.

"Is that what this experience is designed to do, help us forget?" I carefully aimed my words for his heart. They fell like arrows to the ground. My wit left me speechless. They were both stunned by my silence. I was never at a loss for words. My choice of words bore stingers that injected pain, regret and manipulation in the hearts of my victims. But none of that happened and I realized Adam the Second was present.

I stood on the lip of the cave and the sun's rays kissed my face. We stripped off our ponchos and on the count of three, we bolted from the entrance and danced barefoot in the lush grass. I threw my mittens as far as I could, but Meghan ran as hard as she could to collect them before they hit the ground. "No! We'll need these for later." She folded the ponchos and put the mittens in a safe place.

The smell of fresh field greens and fruit toyed with our appetites. To the left of the cave, a small body of water gushed from the waterfall that cascaded over the rocks. Steam from the hot springs reinvigorated my aching back and legs, which hurt from our long walk through the cave. The mountains in the backdrop of the forest served as the perfect palette for our time of relaxation.

We sat down to enjoy the lunch that John had packed for us after relaxing for a while. The bread's aroma captivated our taste buds. Meghan snatched the last piece and joined Ian as they satisfied their ravenous hunger. My sister waved the empty bread bag over my head like a flag. I snatched it away, ready to reprimand them. Faster than a twinkling of an eye, bread tumbled from the bag and did not stop until I turned the bag right side up again. We ate our fill, and then fed the birds and the rest of the animals that dared to come near.

The sunset stood still longer than usual. Ian took that as a sign that it was time for us to go. He checked out the grounds while we packed our things to leave. I stared at the ponchos consideringly. Meghan yelled, "Don't even think about it!"

"What do you mean? It's blazing out here!"

"Because I know what the Second Adam is saying to me. He's telling me we'll need the ponchos again. "Why am I not hearing Him? I'm the oldest."

"You have to listen with your heart. Your heart is too noisy." I folded my arms with displeasure, and sat on the grass to wait for Ian.

Ian had befriended a horse while he was gone and came back riding it bareback. His skills with the animal were quite amazing. While Ian performed tricks with the horse, a St. Bernard dog trotted along side them and joined the act. At first opportunity, I would persuade Ian to bring the horse with us. The horse was large enough for all three of us to ride together. So why not? However, Ian decided that we should bring only one animal along. Well, he overrode my chose of preference. Ian presented his chose of animal to us with a smile. The sleepy-eyed St. Bernard with a canister around its neck, yielded to Ian as he walked the dog over to us. "He's smaller than the horse, so he goes." It made no sense to me at all. I am just along for the walk, I suppose.

Ian tested the dog's strength. The dog galloped along behind Ian, and circled the meadow with Meghan on his back. He stopped in front of me. "Allie, climb aboard." Ian demanded. My mind protested, but I did it anyhow. He lifted Meghan off the beast and said. "He carries weight well. He's going with us."

"Are you crazy? Look how big he is. His paws are the size of saucers...and, and don't forget the amount of food he'd devour." Ian cast his eyes upon the beast.

"You are not the one feeding us. Now are you?" Ian had blasted me good, but I deserved it.

"All right! He goes!"

Meghan danced with the Saint Bernard until she got tired. She decided to name the dog, and I could have sworn it smiled at its name. Who in their right mind would name a one hundred and seventy-five pound dog Twinkle except for Meghan? Again I protested. "Why Twinkle? It's out of character for such a large animal."

"The twinkle in his eyes encourages me to go on. He makes me think of Adam the Second." Yet another answer from Meghan that left me speechless. I was watching my little sister mature before my eyes on our voyage home.

Twinkle was valiant and regal, smart and helpful. Meghan would not have made our first uphill climb without Twinkle. She got along with him better than she would have the horse. Besides that, some of the tight spaces we ventured through were too snug for a horse that size. Ian had been right, and I swallowed my pride and told him so. His embrace was a comfort and it made me more anxious to return home.

Soon it was time to eat again, and I wondered how much Twinkle would put away. Ian made him comfortable while we unpacked. It seemed like a good idea to spread our ponchos over the flat rocks. It was spacious at the top of the hill, and we had a clear view of our surroundings.

"We'll stay here for the night. That is, if that's what you think we should do, Ian."

"Sure. I think that's a fine idea." His smile was so beautiful, just like the smiles of our twin mothers Janet and Jennifer. I had found a new appreciation for my cousin that I never had before.

The calm, clear, breezeless night was perfect for sleeping under the stars. About twenty feet away stood two weather-worn trees that would be good shelter for us. We camped in that spot with Twinkle guarding us throughout the night. The canister that hung around his neck glowed brighter as it got darker. Meghan sang "Twinkle, Twinkle, you are my star, ever shining from afar" until she finally fell asleep.

❖

At the break of day, northern winds picked up speed and whirled through the treetops. We opened our eyes to rolling dark clouds hovering over our heads. The winds were consciously trying to blow us to the far ends of the earth, in hope that our discouragement and fear would keep us from ever leaving the garden. At least, it seemed that way.

The winds alarmed us to quickly pack only what we thought we would need for the journey. Ian loaded Twinkle down with our goods and removed the canister from his neck. The sweet water from the canister took our appetites away, and left us with a boost of energy for the rest of our journey. As we left, Twinkle led the way.

It was not long before we came to a sign that read, 'The Point of No Return'. How chilling was that? The mountain that once served as a beautiful background for our lunch yesterday, closed in on all sides for us to climb. Now we were all alarmed at what the future held for us. Or at least I was.

Ian unpacked Twinkle's burden and Twinkle backed away. We saw nothing more than a few trees dotting the landscape before us. The incline to the top of the mountain had somehow become steeper as we watched. Yours truly was tempted to walk back down the path that had gotten us here. Meghan yelled, "Don't look back!" In my mind, the Second Adam stood behind me blocking the view of what we had left behind. I squared my shoulders, and walked on behind Ian and Twinkle.

Meghan kissed Twinkle on the nose a couple of times, and hugged him, "You've lead us as far as you can go. The twinkle in your eye is gone."

"That may be so," Ian added, "but nevertheless, the Second Adam is still with us." Twinkle faced the sign, and we said our goodbyes. Twinkle watched us walk to the end of the flat rock. Temptation gnawed at me to turn around, until the sound of flapping wings caught my attention.

To our right towered the most elegant butterfly I had ever seen. Its body was crystal clear, and its antennas and wings were opaque, but glittering. Her eyes were sapphires that shone like diamonds.

We climbed a golden ladder between her legs and entered through her belly button. We sat in the glass encasement that made up her stomach. The fairy tale interior transported Meghan's imagination into Cinderella's world. With her imaginary prince by her side, she offered him tea and crumpets. In amazement my emotions accelerated, waiting for something to happen. The winds picked up and suddenly, the butterfly began flying.

During our flight, we talked about home, and about what we would do to make things easier for our mothers. Even after we stopped talking, I was a little too excited to sleep; after all, we were sitting in the stomach of a giant butterfly!

The smooth ride was very enjoyable, until the rough wind created a tear in the butterfly's right wing. My sister began to pray and Ian bowed his head. I reminded them that we were on our way home, no matter what it looked like.

As we prayed for the butterfly (who Meghan had named Missy), she flew lower and lower. Finally a brutal undercurrent of wind snagged her damaged wing. It fluttered helplessly in the wind, and had ripped off of Missy's body entirely. We plummeted downward, but when we hit, we experienced the softest crash that anyone could imagine.

We slid back out of Missy's belly button with ease soon after the crash. Missy whimpered once or twice, and then lay very still. Our backs were against the wind, but Ian fidgeted and dropped our gear a couple of times. He gasped.

"What is it Ian?" I rushed to his side. He panned the circumference of the sky.

"You don't hear it?" Ian pressed his hands against his ears.

"No, I don't hear it." The horror on his face settled somewhat, before he spoke. "The growls I heard in the distance was just the wind. The wind is dying down now." He continued surveying our surroundings after I walked away.

There were many broken tree limbs and a lot of brush scattered about the ground, and Meghan gathered as much of it as she could. I helped cover Missy with the brush to keep her warm. "Ian!" He profiled me. "Why aren't you helping us cover Missy? The faster we get done, the faster we can run to safety!" Meghan stroked Missy with love. "This is a big butterfly, you know." Ian walked over to us without saying a word. He fidgeted as he looked over his shoulder.

After covering Missy, our next problem was to figure out where we could stay the night to avoid the stinging winds. We had only been traveling inside Missy for around six hours. How could we go from having a wonderful time in the sun, to chilling winds and God knows what else in such a short period of time? My sister never ceased to call out for help from the higher power in her life.

"Well," Ian proclaimed, "we had a safe time with Missy while it lasted."

"Rest her little soul." Meghan replied.

"Hey guys, where's our food? Our blankets and ponchos are gone too!" Ian spoke up before I could go on with my search.

"Angry Winds took them." Ian quietly replied.

"What?"

"Don't worry. The Second Adam will get them back."

CHAPTER ELEVEN

Forced Entry

It grew darker by the minute as furious winds continued to blow. We needed a place to lay our heads for the evening, with Missy out of sight and no dinner. Ian and I shielded Meghan against flying debris as much as possible to keep her safe. We could not hold up much longer. It was unbelievable to see the force of wind suck the leaves off of a tree that stood in our path.

We could not help but notice a huge tree hundreds of years old that was completely undisturbed by the wind. Not even the leaves or the branches swayed. The tree roots were deep, and its branches touched the earth. Angry Winds inhaled deeply. Gusts of winds released from its cheeks spun us around to face the tree. The tree opened its mouth wide; it was toothless. I realized that just meant it would take longer for us to die. Hopelessly, I closed my eyes and waited to feel the tree's first bite.

At high velocity, in a moment's time, we descended down. It was like riding a giant slide at a high rate of speed. Sparks flew when we tumbled inside the tree. Ian landed on the sofa, and Meghan was sitting in an upright position on a chair. I ended up on the floor, sitting in front of the fireplace. When we came to ourselves, we were astounded at the beauty of the tree's interior. The storm was over for us, thanks to Adam the Second and His treehouse.

Our ponchos hung on wall hooks to my right. Everything that Angry Winds had taken from us was sitting on the floor below our ponchos. In a reflective mood, I took Meghan's place on the chair near the fireplace. My little sister rushed to the dinner table, without delay. Ian and Meghan gave thanks for the provisions made and began eating. I hung my head, and gave a quiet thanks to the Second Adam.

A familiar touch on my shoulder excited me. "Adam the Second." Ian and Meghan thanked Him for coming.

"I never left you." He received Meghan's embrace. "Meghan, Missy's fine. She's not as fragile as you think. She's with my friend John."

"Yesssss!" Meghan shook both fists in delight.

"Now, I would like to hear your thoughts about your journey this far."

"Yes sir." Meghan stopped eating and sat at attention. "God's power has been with us through everything we've had to face. It's been scary, but we made it. I love you."

"I love you too, Meghan. And you, Ian?"

"Sir, I have never experienced such wisdom in my life. I appreciate the Spirit of God's wisdom."

"It's always available to you. You must remain open to it." I could almost see Ian's heart reflecting on the words that Adam the Second had just spoken to him. "That leaves you Allison." "I have a question." "Sure, ask anything you want."

"When will we get home?" My sister and cousin winced.

"You're almost there. The last test is the most challenging. I will speak to each of you individually while you're here."

"Yes sir." I said, hoping it would not take too long. I missed every aspect of home, and did not want to stay in the tree house longer than necessary. My own bed and bathtub would suit me just fine.

The Second Adam had heard me, although I had not spoken those words aloud. Running to hide after thinking such a thing would have been the appropriate thing to do. He had been so good to us. I was unappreciative and selfish and He knew that. His gaze burned deep inside me, and I hung my head in shame.

We whispered among ourselves and promised to share with each other, whatever Adam the Second would share with us. Meghan said she would never forget the evening of the first night, we spent with Adam the Second in the treehouse.

"Meghan, this way to my office, shall we?" He pointed the way. After Meghan returned from her talk with Adam, she told me everything that had transpired.

"It's always a pleasure to talk to you, Adam the Second." She said, sitting down across from Him.

"God loves you so much."

"Oh, believe me, I feel it every day."

"Meghan, God is love. He simply wants to give His love to someone. It is for anyone who will accept it." She nodded.

Her words had flowed from her as she looked at the portrait that hung on the wall in front of them.

"God's love always makes me want to love someone else. Everyone needs to know about His love. I learned that from you." She gave a girlish giggle and crossed her legs. "That's spoken from the heart of a true disciple of God."

"You mean someone who trusts and believes the Good Shepherd."

"Yes."

Still she had gazed intently at the portrait stretched across the fireplace. Liquid pain flooded her eyes and flushed her cheeks. "Why does he hate me so? All I want to do is love my dad." The Second Adam opened his arms to her, and lifted her chin with His index finger. "Look at the portrait again."

The portait was one of Meghan, sitting on her father's lap. "Did my mother make him take the picture with me?" "No, he was willing."

"Why doesn't he live with us, then?"

"Things happen because of the choices people make. Look at me, Meghan." She had seen the love in His eyes that He had for her, and He felt her pain. "Whenever you look at that portrait, see Me in him. Pray for him. He needs it. See Me. My love is sure and life-changing."

"I will. I promise I will. I will see you in everything I do."

"Are you sure about that?"

"Very. I trust you."

Meghan had leaned closer to the portrait, and gasped when she saw Adam the Second's face instead of Dad's. Adam the Second's pleasant chuckles had turned into side splitting laughter that echoed throughout every room of the tree house. He had prayed for Meghan, and had eaten cheese and fruit with her.

I noticed Ian from the corner of my eye. He nodded at me like an old fat bull in a green pasture, all alone and loving it. He threw his feet upon the ottoman in front of the chair. In no time at all, his head fell backward and his tongue lolled against his bottom lip, and he was out like a light. However I should not be so hard on him. His valiant efforts had totally drained the life out of him. He deserved the restful sleep he was having. A yawn escaped my lips and the coziness of the fire drew me in, as I decided to join Ian in slumber.

"Allison! Allison!" The voice was more desperate with each scream. Unlike in the cave, warm winds now surrounded me. I had no idea where I was or what I was supposed to be doing.

Did my speaking out of turn about leaving the treehouse so soon cause this? If I had not spoken out of turn, perhaps I would still be cozying up by the fire.

My living nightmare helplessly floated me through the darkness. An unintelligible voice mumbled. Finally able to speak aloud myself, my question flung itself at her. "Who are you?"

"Allison, help me!" Cayleigh's desperation heightened mine. "Where are you?" She grabbed my ankle.

"No! Please let go of me!" I wriggled to get free. I tried smashing her fingers with my other foot. "Let go, or else you'll take me down with you!"

"Please!" Pain surged through my ankle, and up the calf of my leg. Her heavy breathing was just as oppressive as the darkness around us.

Just as I was about to give up, Meghan's laughter brought me back to reality. Ian had woken up as well, and went to the bathroom to straighten himself up for his interview with the Second Adam. "Allison, are you all right?" Adam the Second asked. I responded with a quick nod. My heart still throbbed, and the sweat on my brow should have told Him something. Meghan came from the kitchen with a cold glass of water.

"Why not move away from the fireplace if you're too warm?"

I managed a smile. "I'm fine." I lay there with my eyes closed thinking about the dream and how real it had felt.

The massage to the stinging pain in my leg was of no comfort at all. My ankle was red and swollen where fingers had held on. My little sister came from the kitchen with ice cubes wrapped in a paper towel. "Do you see this Meghan?" She handed me the ice without a word. I laid it across my ankle without saying thank you and closed my eyes again.

I was incredibly frustrated by the smile that graced Meghan's face. Meghan had the I-can't-help-its ever since her encounter with the Second Adam. Her smile was beautiful though. My sister had always had Mom's graceful walk and charitable ways. Dad's disposition and facial features had always been my makeup. Is it so bad to be like your biological father? I supposed that was a question for Adam the Second to answer.

Just like Meghan, Ian told me everything that had transpired when he had spoken with Adam the Second. Ian followed the Second Adam into the other room. At the touch of the Second Adam's calloused hands on Ian's shoulders, Ian's exhaustion vanished instantly. Without delay, Ian thanked Him for being loyal to him.

I did not see what everyone else sees in the Second Adam. Well, I just did not see it. I would love to be more in love with Him than the first night I met Him on the beach, but... I suppose I would figure it out after I talked to Him. I hoped my conversation with this man would not be a lengthy one. I did not want to say or do anything that would delay my progress in getting home.

Ian had waited beside his chair until Adam the Second was seated. The photo on the desk had showed Ian standing next to the Second Adam, looking like a distinguished young man on the rise. Ian was posing in front of the mansion as if he owned it. He gloated in amazement at how refined and mature he looked standing next to the Second Adam.

The Second Adam had finished a glass of apricot nectar while Ian surveyed the room and its bookshelves. Dozens of books had been neatly arranged on a table near the window. His fingers had danced along the spine of the set of reference books that rested on the desk. The young man's desire for the book world had always meant more to him than his relationship with God.

The Second Adam had added another log to the fire. "Why read, if there is no positive influence gained from what you are reading? Do you know what happens to you when you read and study worthless material?" Ian had slid his hands into his pockets. "You become what you read. And if your reading material is worthless, you try to hide the truth." Ian had stared at the flames without a word. "And then what you have, my friend, is an effective hypocrite."
Ian nodded. "I agree wholeheartedly."

The painting over the fireplace had suddenly flashed back into time, to the garden with the destructive bookworm that had brought him there. "I've got you right where I want you." The gravelly voice boasted. "Pornography is the hardest material for a young man to put down, you know."

"Leave me alone!"

"It's too late for that now." The worm said as it swallowed him.

"Help! Help me, somebody!" Ian pounded his fist on the sides of the worm's belly. "Let me go!" He thought about Jonah in the belly of the whale. He wondered if he was running from God just as Jonah had. The thought made Ian sick, and he threw up onto the vomit that already rested in the worm's belly.

"Before you know it, I will have you believing that your God is as powerless as a gnat in the Atlantic Ocean!" His laughter rang throughout the valley as he regurgitated Ian from his stomach. Ian slid on the ground to the edge of the grass among the trees. "This is far enough. They'll find you here. See you later, stupid."

The scene had faded from the huge painting that hung over the fireplace. Ian had spat in the fire, remembering that day. But that was not the end of what he had needed to contend with.

Next, the portrait had unveiled his deepest, darkest, secret that no one else knew about.

"You know, your mother found the magazines."

Ian's eyes bounced all around the room and back to Adam the Second.

"What?"

"I allowed her to." His knees buckled and the ebook he held in his hand fell to the floor.

Ian had been too ashamed to look at the Second Adam. He had walked across the room to the window. Without hesitation, the window pane had picked up where the portrait had left off.

Ian's long weekend of study had paid off. He had already passed his journalism class with flying colors. The calculus exam was the next exam of the day. He approached his locker, and reached for the combination lock. Students in the hallway gathered around. Some giggled. Others whispered. It was such a strange feeling to have everyone watching. After all, he was just performing the simple task of unlocking his locker.

When he opened his locker, pornographic magazines poured out and covered the floor. The brass-faced hall monitor gingerly removed the alcoholic beverage that occupied the corner of the locker. Eventually, the hall monitors cleared the halls, and calmed the crowd. When the last bell of the day rang, the hall monitor escorted Ian to the principal's office. The office assistant that followed them carried the evidence with a twisted smile.

Although Ian welcomed the relief he had felt from the last bell ringing, he could not escape his surroundings quickly enough. He just wanted to go home and hide from those who occupied his world. To justify his innocence, names and faces coursed through his mind. Who would do such a thing?

To his chagrin, two law enforcement officers waited at the office door to escort him away from the premises. Ian was suspended from school for the rest of the year and would not graduate.

Roderick and Tyler peeked around the corner near the office. As the police rounded the corner with Ian, Roderick and Tyler embraced the glass showcase displaying Ian's academic awards for school representation. They saluted him with pity as he walked by.

Word had gotten out about his habit, and spread like wildfire. Ian had become the laughing stock of the school and the community at large. Not to mention his shame at home and church. In his heart he knew that he had been set up by his friends. They were jealous of his intelligence, and this was how they repaid him.

"How could this happen to me? I'm a double A honor student!" The emotions he felt was so real. Adam the Second reminded him that this would be his fate if he did not change his ways.

Ian had still been looking at the painting when he heard the singing. He had noticed the painting's similarities to the mural at the hotel. Only this time, the little girl had looked like Meghan. She was holding her mother's hand, and her father was standing close by, smiling. Ian's mother was there with him, too. Everyone was present in the portrait except - you guessed it – Allison.

"Will Allison make it?" Adam the Second had given a half nod in response to Ian's question. Ian returned to his seat, blinded by his tears.

CHAPTER TWELVE

Spiritual Reality Check

Ian had grabbed the box of tissue Adam the Second offered him. Thirty minutes of hard weeping had left him breathless, but at the Second Adam's embrace, the tears ceased and Ian breathed deeply. "Why didn't you do that in the first place? I was totally out of control."

"You needed very much to pour out your emotions. My embrace was merely provided closure." "Thank you. I don't know what I would do without you." A weak smile occupied his face.

"Son, the choices you make now will affect your future in every way."

Ian had toyed with the soaked tissues in his hand. "What do you mean?"

"Your college curriculum choices will affect your occupation, who you marry and how you communicate with your children." Ian had reflected on the Second Adam's wisdom with a fixed gaze.

"There is a constant struggle between the world of darkness and the world of light. The struggle is for control of the souls of men. Ian you will walk away from me completely if your philosophy of life ever overpowers your spiritual understanding." The blood drained from Ian's face. Licking his dry lips, he swallowed hard.

He had explained the deceptions that would vy for Ian's attention. The Second Adam had exhaled a sigh of tension. "Be careful of what you read and believe." Ian had denied in his heart that he would ever fall prey to those deceptions, until he thought about the story of a fisherman named Peter.

Officers, religious people, and servants drudged through the garden with torches, lanterns and weapons. His follower looked past Him and pressed his lips against His cheek. "Judas, you betray me with a kiss?"

"Lord, shall we fight with the sword?" Before he could respond, with one swipe of his sword, Peter severed off the right ear of the high priest's servant whose name was Malchus.

Blood ran down Malchus' neck. However, the accused gave no charge for battle.

"Put your sword away!" The Lord retrieved the severed ear and laid His hand on the side of the wounded servant's face. The bleeding stopped. "Shall I not drink what is mine?"

Warmth clung to Malchus' face where the accused had laid his hand. Stopped in his tracks by the Lord's love, Malchus checked his ear. Not only had the bleeding stopped, there was no sign that the ear had ever been severed, and his hearing was even clearer than before. Soldiers nudged him out of the way to make the arrest. But his eyes were locked on the accused. He suddenly knew that an innocent man full of love was being arrested. And for what?

Peter stepped aside to let the soldiers carrying torches pass by. In the darkness, he scooped up a handful of leaves to wipe the blood from his short sword. He thrust the bloody leaves behind him, and dabbed at his wet eyes with the forearm of his sleeve.

The guards that surrounded Jesus knocked Him to His knees. His hands were roped behind Him. Yet His disciples abided by His command, and did not retaliate with fighting.

Confused and afraid, Peter forced his sword back into its sheath as he rushed from the garden to the courtyard. The soldiers beckoned him to follow along behind them as they approached the palace.

The other follower with Peter was well acquainted with Caiphas. Caiphas had served in the office of the priesthood that year, and had resided in the palace at the time of Jesus' ministry. The other follower entered the palace with the accused, while Peter waited in the courtyard. However, the young palace doorkeeper recognized Peter as one of the Galilean followers. When he was challenged about that, Peter flatly denied having had any dealings with the man.

In the courtyard, the servants and officers warmed themselves around a fire. The rustic fisherman joined them, hoping to remain inconspicuous even though he was dressed like a Galilean. His eyes furtively darted from face to face. The stench of his own breath entered his nostrils.

"Hey, aren't you one of his students?"

"I am not!" The answer came faster than he could think.

One of Malchus' relatives stood across from Peter. He recognized Peter's clothes. "Didn't I see you in the garden?" Peter cursed profusely as he gave his third and final denial. A cock crowed, and he fled in terror.

Falling at the Second Adam's feet, Ian had cradled his little finger in the nail scar in His wrist. "Please, tell me, what do I have to do to keep from denying you?"

Adam the Second had helped him to his feet. "Hear my words, always meditate on them and love me with all of your heart. Talk to me as often as you think about me. I will always answer you one way or another."

"I will."

"It's not just you, son." He helped Ian to the chair in front of the desk.

"So, meditating on your words and acting upon them and prayer, is spiritual maintenance?"

"Once again my son, that is exactly right."

"Darkness is after Allison's soul, but she's going to make it."

"I am relieved to know that." Adam the Second had leaned forward and rested his hand on Ian's. "Some people must learn the hard way, and she is one of those people."

"Why don't they hurry up?" I pounded the arm of the chair with my fist, punctuating each word with a strike. Meghan sat at attention during my outburst. "They will finish when it's time."

A hush came over me, and the slippery darkness wrapped its slithering arms around me once more.

The darkness clung to my body like slimy serpents. "Wake up, Allison! Wake up!" I screamed to myself. I thanked God that at least Ian and Meghan were safe even as my own strength waned. I desperately needed help, but did not know where to turn.

To my amazement, pockets of light slid down the sides of the tunnel.

CayLeigh's voice echoed. "Those beams of light are your mother's prayers. You are riding on her prayers."

"CayLeigh! It can be different for you, too. You'll see." CayLeigh did not answer me. She could not hear me, no matter how loudly I screamed. If I could not help her, how could I help myself? What was going to happen once I reached the bottom of the tunnel? I braced myself for the worst.

Through the dimness of the tunnel, a faint image stood below me. Looking past the light, Adam the Second stood with his arms open wide. To fall into His arms at the rate of speed in which I was traveling would have been pure luck. It was worth a try to angle myself toward Him and hope for the best.

Adam the Second withdrew His arms as I plummeted past Him. Headed straight for a raging sea of molten lava, I screamed for mercy. Trickles of light pulled themselves from the sides of the tunnel, forming small tornadoes. The tornadoes swirled together, and merged into one giant tornado of light. It spread across the lake of molten lava, creating a web of light that broke my fall just in time. I screamed with frantic joy. "Thank God for mother's prayers, mother's prayers, mother's prayers, mother's prayers!"

When I came to myself I was off the chair and in Second Adam's arms. My throat ached from screaming. He spoke softly to me, and I regained my composure. Meghan was crouched down and peeking at me from behind a chair. Ian crouched behind the Second Adam, holding a sword that no longer occupied its shaft near the fireplace.

Adam the Second stroked strands of tear soaked hair from my eyes, and pushed it away from my face. "Are you ready for your instructions?"
"Yes I am. Thank you."

He pointed toward His office. Still visibly shaken, the Second Adam steadied me as I plopped down on the chair and He left the room as the face of the painting over the fireplace had changed again. This time, it portrayed a young woman with age lines that creased the outline of her face. Crow's feet perched the corners of her eyes.

There were five young children in the painting. Three looked exactly like the woman, but the two larger children in the portrait had no faces or limbs. Quite disturbed by the painting, I could hardly contain my emotions.

Adam the Second entered the room and sat down, but I remained unaware of His presence. I ran my hand across the woman's face, and strained my memory to place her in my life.

The Second Adam cleared his throat. "What do you see, Allison?"

"How long have you been sitting there?"

"Oh, about forty-five minutes." I could not tell if I was more disturbed by the portrait or the fact that I had not recognized Adam's presence in the room. We sat in silence for about thirty more minutes. Finally I spoke.

"I'm confused about all this. What do the faceless children mean? And who is the mother?"

"As a matter of fact, you know her quite well. But not as well as you're about to." At those words, the wrinkles, crow's feet and the hardness disappeared from her face.

"It's CayLeigh! What happened to her? Why are the two older children faceless?" The Second Adam waited for my conclusion.

"Could it possibly mean that they are unborn? But that makes no sense. Their bodies are larger than the other three."

"It's worse. It means that CayLeigh had two abortions."

"That's murder."

"Try telling her that."

"But can't she be stopped before this happens?"

"She needs someone praying for her daily. She needs to give her life to the Good Shepherd. He's the only one that can help her." The Second Adam abruptly cut our conversation short, and walked me to the door. I forgot all about asking Him about the molten lava nightmare.

"Prepare yourself for home. You will only need the clothes on your back."

"We're that close?" He kissed me on the forehead. "You're that close. After a good night's rest and a good hearty breakfast, you will be on your way." I smoothed the wrinkles out of Meghan's blouse and laid it on the back of the sofa next to mine and within seconds sank into peaceful slumber.

CHAPTER THIRTEEN

River Rage

The next morning, Ian entered the room focused and ready to face the consequences in going home. What could Adam the Second have said to produce such courage in him? Cous kissed me on the cheek and sat down to breakfast. My little sister said grace before speaking to anyone.

"Are you ready for the journey home?" I rejected the smile Meghan offered me.

"I suppose so." I replied. "Has Adam given you your instructions yet?" I looked at Ian, then at Meghan, and back to Ian again.

"He will when He's ready." She popped her answer with finesse.

"That's up to Him." He answered without taking his eyes off of his plate.

Adam the Second had not given instructions regarding our journey as of yet. Well, at least, not to me. I had prepared myself for the worst.

Ian daubed at the corners of his mouth with his napkin after a delightful breakfast. He pushed himself from the table, ready for the journey ahead. John came to dispose of our things.

We had no butterfly, no dog, or birds to tag along for support or guidance. Fortunately, I did not care about any of that. Nor did I try to hide my eagerness to leave the tree house.

From a distance, the Second Adam gestured to us to be on our way. He never said goodbye. He never smiled or offered to walk us to the path that we should take. He just whistled as we followed the grassland to the narrow, crooked path that Ian chose. I got cold feet just looking at the trail underneath the open sky. The path led to the north side of the garden.

We set off, placing one foot before the other along the crooked path. Ian and Meghan kept their heads held high to keep from looking down into the ravine along the path. Their trust in the Second Adam was phenomenal. I wondered what made me so different from them.

Ian sensed my fear and placed my hand on his belt loop. My little sister marched along fearlessly behind me. None of us spoke a word.

Despite my fear, the scenery was certainly beautiful. The valley was cool and breezy and rays of sunlight eased through the thick trees. The shadows in the valley had paralyzed travelers with fear. Some travelers lay near us heaving on the ground, unable to walk. They would never reach their destination.

The shadows became smaller as we continued our journey. Ian called for a short break - a time of reflection, he called it. I was not tired, but followed his word. What could it hurt? The journey had become a learning experience. I felt much better about myself.

We came to the edge of a small river that appeared harmless. "I think we should cross the river at its narrowest point." With a nod of the head, and a folding of the arms, my posture glared finality.

Ian disagreed with me.
"I think we should cross it in the middle." He firmly stated.
"Crossing the midpoint will take longer." I argued.

"Yes, but we have huge rocks to climb over and go around at the lowest point." Ian nearly wacked my nose when he pointed in the direction of the rocks. I swatted at his finger and continued yelling,

"Yeah but, the water is deeper in the middle of the river." I moved him closer to the edge of the river to prove my point.

"Yeah, but it's calmer. Allison."

"God forbid that one of us should fall into the river!" Ian took one giant step toward me. "Don't humor me!" He pushed his eyeglasses securely against the bridge of his nose, and stood toe to toe with me. He argued his point so passionately, spit flew from his mouth.

Ian re-adjusted his glasses, straightened his clothes, and said, "The middle of the river is safer!"

"Safer for me and you, maybe. Ian, you never want to do things my way!"

"Allison, all our lives are at stake here. We have to do what's best for everyone."

"I agree with Ian, Allie."

Unconvinced about Ian's answer, I shook my head. His body language spoke loud and clear, but he said, "All right, cous. Have it your way. The narrowest point of the river awaits us." The waters calmly bounced as Ian watched.

Suddenly, uneasy about my decision, I had to stand my ground. I had to fight for what I wanted or lose everything the way I had lost Dad. We faced the river's narrowest point. Ian and Meghan kissed and hugged each other. "This is not the time for that. We're trying to get home." Meghan smiled at me and lovingly touched my hand, but her eyes betrayed her nervousness.

Meghan slipped her foot into the water, and mumbled Adam the Second's name. She leaped to get to the second rock, and clung to it as soon as she landed. Suddenly, the waters began to swell as the river enlarged itself. By the time Meghan reached the center of the river, she could not go any further nor could she go back to the river's edge. The violent water licked its lips at the prospect of its innocent victim.

"Oh my God!" I shrieked, the river has turned on us!"

"Hang on, Meghan!" Ian yelled, "don't let go!" He ran closer to the bank. A branch hung from a tree near the river's edge. He swung on the branch, and held it down as close to the river as he could. "Grab the branch. It'll hold your weight."

"Allie! Help!" I could not move for fear. I had done it again. I was right back to square one. How stupid, stupid, stupid I had been!

The force of the waves pulled Meghan's hands away from the rock she was clinging to. Ian held a branch over the river waiting for her to float in his direction. However, the river abruptly shifted into a sharp zigzag course, and Meghan passed by Ian altogether. Fortunately, Meghan's head stayed above water through it all. I could still hear her panic-filled screams.

The deafening roar of falling water announced the presence of a waterfall. "Second Adam, save me! Please! I need you!" It was my fault that my sister was calling for Adam the Second. I ran to catch up with Ian unable to cope with that at the moment. The look on his face filled me with shame and guilt all over again, and I backed away from him to the edge of the river. Suddenly, a cloudburst settled directly above us. It was impossible to get to Meghan now. Standing helplessly in drenching rains, we could only watch as Meghan floated past and helplessly disappeared from sight.

My need to always be right had killed my little sister. So what else was left for me to do except take my own life? I was sure Mom could survive my death easier than Meghan's. I would not want to live without my sister. Once she hit the waterfall, it would be over for her. There were too many rocks in the river for her to avoid every single one on her way down. So from that moment on, my decision was to take my life.

The roar of the waterfall almost sounded like cruel laughter as Meghan approached the falls. "I've got you now." "You won't make it out alive!"

"Second Adam," Meghan cried just before she reached the waterfall's edge, "You are here. I know You are!" She failed in her efforts to dog paddle, and closed her eyes for the drop-off over the falls.

Unexpectedly, a rainbow appeared in the sky and a small, beautiful being with wings and long legs appeared above the river. Music emanated from her wings and filled the air. I don't believe in fairies, but that was the only word I thought of that could classify this petite creature. She quietly called Meghan's name. "I am Isabella, your Crusader. Just relax. Reach for me. You can do it."

Meghan reached for Isabella's hand, and Isabella waved her other hand over Meghan's feet. Meghan stood on her tippy toes on the river with her right hand extended toward heaven. "Come on now, you know what to do."

Meghan danced on the waves and made them calm down. Isabella joined her in the dance.

Their leaps and turns and plie's were absolutely breathtaking. Meghan flew and danced in the middle of the sky and kissed the rainbow. Vibrant neon colors flashed across the sky.

The girls leaped above the river and twirled from treetop to treetop. Finally, Meghan spectacularly returned to the river, with Isabella by her side. The waves calmed down, and the river returned to normal everywhere they placed their feet.

Isabella glanced in the direction of the rainbow. Meghan nodded in agreement. "Wait a minute," I thought, perplexed and standing on my tippy toes, "What is she agreeing to?" Too much was happening too soon. Ian could not take his eyes off Isabella and Meghan. Tears filled my eyes, although I was too stubborn to let them fall.

Isabella ascended higher into the air above the waterfall, still holding my little sister's hand. They glided up until they were once again level with the rainbow. The girls danced on the rainbow until they disappeared. I instantly became sick to my stomach. This was just great. I was on my way home, but with no sister to show for it!

The rainbow slowly dissipated from the atmosphere like fine, wispy vapor. Moreover, the landscape had lost all beauty in my eyes, and the river's new tranquility devastated me. The sun shone brightly as if nothing had ever happened.

Ian's sorrow reached me before he did. He stopped to pick up the bag of snacks Meghan dropped to the ground on her way to cross the river. Therefore we continued our journey in silence. If I had listened to Ian my footsteps would not have been loaded with grief. Even more importantly, my sister would still be here. It made no sense to me why Adam the Second had not come to her defense.

CHAPTER FOURTEEN

Escape from Wormwood Village

Just as the sun was rising, we reached a prairie landscape. Coyotes hiding among the rocks howled when they saw us. We were filled with paranoia, as we crossed the desert in plain view of anything watching. There was no place to hide.

I could not help but stub my toes on the rocks scattered all about on the ground. Trinkets and sequins that had once adorned my ballet slip-ons lay in the dust behind us. Blood seeped through the holes in my shoes, and Ian laughed. This just added to the silence between us, which was choking the life right out of me. Ian's behavior convinced me that he would never forgive me for my sister's disappearance with Isabella.

Strange moisture-filled breezes occasionally whistled past us, apparently intending to keep us hydrated. They certainly helped refresh us from our last ordeal.

In the middle of the desert, we found a cove of trees hidden in a deep fog. The breeze tightened its grip on us, and propelled us towards the cove. I struggled with the breeze, but refused to let on to Ian that I was afraid.

"Watch your head!" Ian barked as I walked underneath the trees. Worms were hanging from the trees like apples. Little growls were coming from the worms, and a repulsive odor from the digusting liquid oozed from their mouths.

Slime hung from the trees like holiday garland hanging from a Christmas tree. Without a doubt, it came from the cocoons we saw all over the trees. Ian led the way with slime coating his glasses. We had to crawl on our stomachs to avoid getting completely covered by the slime; it hung so low on some trees. What a fine mess we were in - all because of me.

Ian spoke over his shoulder to me. "Nothing you say can help us now. But we will survive." His countenance had changed. He looked determined and his candor ignited sparks of courage inside me. I lay breathless on the ground. Listening to Ian at that moment was like listening to Adam the Second all over again. His tone of voice, the cadence, even the volume...they all matched the Second Adam's perfectly. It would help if only I could keep that in mind as we faced challenging situations in the future.

As we continued crawling, leaves from the trees and the slime from the worm cocoons formed an enclosed tunnel around us. We must have crawled nearly half a mile before coming to any light.

The worms crawled out from among the leaves that were scattered across the ground. We crawled as fast as we could through the narrow tunnel to escape the worms. The disgusting smell of the worms' saliva made me cough hard enough to vomit.

Finally, we broke through to fresh air. We could not crawl fast enough towards the soft green wall erected in front of us. "Look!" Ian jumped to his feet and ran. Strange sounds shook the wall. I bounced off the green wall, and slipped on slime underfoot. I scrambled to my feet to catch up with Ian.

The bookworm was hunched over, and antennas erupted through the pores of his skin on top of his head. He used the antennas as some kind of radar to locate us, and it looked like his red eyes could follow the heat of our bodies. The bookworm transmitted our location to the rest of the worms in the village.

We saw large, military-looking worms guarding the birthing stations of Wormwood Village. Just inside the city limits of Wormwood Village were holes burrowed deeply inside the ground that seemed to serve as channels for the birthing stations. They were well hidden among the coves of trees in the area which would provide them with good cover from birds of prey who would otherwise feed off the young.

Their homes were simple red clay mounds that led to underground living quarters. It looked like the male worms took turns standing guard during the night in front of their territory.

A few of the worms that lived in the village appeared almost human-like. They had regular teeth and ears on the sides of their heads, and necklines. Their personalities showed compassion and bravery when needed. Other worms had buck-tooth fangs, and appeared prideful about the stingers they possessed on the tips of their tails.

The transmission from the chief raced throughout Wormwood Village, bringing it to a blur of chaotic activity. Worms raced towards us, hopping on the tips of their tails like baby kangaroos.

During all of the commotion, I lost sight of Ian. "Ian, where are you?"

"Allison, up here!" The bookworm holding Ian by the collar, threw his head back and laughed. Ian yelled for Adam the Second. The sky flickered. In haste, the worm threw Ian over his head, and swallowed him in one gulp. It licked its lips and patted its stomach. "Hm, good." It said. The splashing around after he swallowed Ian must have been the worm's stomach fluids. Horrified by it all and in shock, I waited for the worm to devour me as well.

The sky flickered a second time. Smoke shot through the sky. When the smoke cleared, the words, James the third, Crusader of the Second Adam, flamed across the sky. Suddenly, the young crusader shot out from behind a cloud, and floated in midair on a skateboard. He used his radar vision to identify the leader of the worm village. The young lad skateboarded through the sky, bouncing from cloud to cloud, until he hovered directly over the head of the bookworm that had swallowed Ian.

I could not believe what I had just witnessed. The bookworm opened its mouth, and James the Crusader bravely raced straight into it. The worm gulped him down, and turned to slither back toward the village.

"Hang on, Ian. The fun has just begun." Ian grabbed onto James the Crusader's belt, and the crusader used the turbo boost in his shoes to race up and down the worm's esophagus. "This is more fun than any roller coaster. Stir your foot around in his stomach acid, and then yank it out real fast." Ian did, and the worm groaned as soon as Ian jerked his foot away. The worm's stomach juices sloshed high, almost reaching the boys. "He'll throw up if you do it again!"

"I don't think I want to try that."

"Have you ever tickled a worm's nose before?"

"Nope, this'll be the first time!" Ian snickered.

James the Crusader took Ian to the inside of the worm's nose. "Blow on these as hard as you can."

"These two little bumps right here?"

"Mm-hmm." James nodded.

"The harder you blow, the more severe the sneeze."

"Should I let him have it?"

"Let him have it!" Ian blew hard enough to become lightheaded. His boyish chuckle with James the Crusader's echoed from the worm just before it opened its mouth to sneeze.

I was unaware of what was happening inside the worm's body, but I could certainly see the aftermath. The worm clutched its ears and held its head. Its stomach was moving in and out, and retching noises hurled from its mouth. I moved far away from the worm. Its face twitched from side to side, and spittle ran down the side of its jaw. The worm opened its mouth and wrinkled its nose. James said. "On the count of three, do it!"

"One, two, three - now, Ian!" Ian let the bookworm have it, with all the breath he could muster. James the Crusader helped Ian back to his feet just as the bookworm opened its mouth. The bright light hurt his eyes. James the third, Crusader of Adam and Ian stood on the worm's tongue and looked at the ground, and Ian whimpered when he saw the distance to the ground.

"Ian there's one thing you must do for me once we're on the ground."
"And that is?"
"Gather as much of the dried cocoon slime as you can. Tie the ends together."
"Where should I put it?"
"Lay it beside the jet-ski after I park it."
"Yes sir." He saluted the super hero, and vowed immediate action.

By this time the chief worm had worked up a good sneeze. James the Crusader said. "Close your eyes and hold your breath."
"And then what?"
"Hold on to my belt and don't let go."
"You don't have to worry about me. I am not Allison." The worm's deep breath enlarged his stomach as these words were spoken.

He blew Ian and James the third, Crusader of Adam out of its nostrils and onto the ground. James the Crusader stood tall, with Ian cradled in his arms. Ian leaped from the crusader's arms. "Man, that was fly. It was so exhilarating!"

"I thought you'd like it. Nostrils are always fun, especially without all the goo."

"With speed like that man...with speed like that, it would have been impossible for anything to hang on."

The chief had collapsed down onto the ground. The tip of his tail curled and his eyes were crossed. The entire village of worms bounced on their tails and hooted at their chief, encouraging him to get up and go on. His family gathered around him, and loved him back to life.

The chief flinched as he came to, knowing he had to face James the third, Crusader of Adam.

The worm looked around for James the Crusader, but could not find him. After some time searching, the worm fell to the ground again with his arms by his side. His fists opened slowly, and he stopped moving. There were no signs of life, and the worms from the village gathered to mourn. Eventually, the worms went their separate ways. They travelled back to the entrance of their village and prepared to attack all trespassers.

"James Crusader of Adam, we won." Ian backed up slowly, and kicked at the worm's body. "You thought you outsmarted us, didn't you? Come on out, James the Crusader boy!"

"No, Ian!" I screamed. Ian stood near the chief's open hand. As he kicked, he tripped over the worm's finger and fell into the palm of its hand. The fist closed around Ian's body and the worm rose from the ground, obviously not dead at all.

James the third, Crusader of the Second Adam, suddenly appeared again. He loudly announced the need for a cloud, which he called by the name Ecclesia-Don. He told the sun and the other crusaders to join him later. The storm cloud Ecclesia-Don, immediately hung over his head, and instantly transformed into a jet-ski before my very eyes. James the Crusader boarded the jet-ski and floated through the air in front of the worm. The worm darted back and forth around him and attempted to knock him off of his jet-ski. The worm's efforts were completely unsuccessful, and the worm had even fewer options left.

The bookworm had not reckoned with James the Crusader's speed, or his bravery. He jumped off the jet-ski cloud and spun around several times in midair. The worm opened its mouth, ready for a salty little boy snack. James the third, Crusader of the Second Adam evaded the worm's lunge, and ran up the worm's body and dived off its nose. The fearless crusader grabbed his jet-ski with both hands, and used his body weight to swing back and forth underneath it. He used his legs to pummel the worm's jaws relentlessly, while hanging onto the jet-ski. I could not tell where his kicks began or ended, his legs moved so swiftly.

The worm weaved back and forth. It came at James the Crusader with fury. It swung left and right, cursing him in its native worm language. That was the last straw for this youth of bravery. James the Crusader jet-skied up the length of the bookworm's arm; it swatted at him numerous times, unsuccessfully. The worm reached for the crusader wonder boy and in a flash, James the third, Crusader of the Second Adam roped the chief's arms down by his side using the dried slime Ian had collected. The chief worm aimlessly hopped from side to side. It inhaled deeply, trying to break the dried cocoon slime. James tightened his grip on the slime as the worm inhaled. The chief's head grew larger with each breath until its ruby eyes disintergrated, streaming red fluid that covered its face.

The relentless crusader parked the jet-ski. He pressed the digital button on his crusader belt to reactivate his turbo shoes that left him standing two feet above the ground. Within a matter of seconds, he wound the dried slime ropes around the chief's tail and flew around in a circle at the speed of light within a matter of seconds. The chief book-worm's head exploded, and rained green slime just outside Wormwood Village. I ran for cover among the trees.

The worms had a huge army of reinforcements beneath the ground, just waiting for their leader's command to attack. James the Crusader gave the command in their native worm language and the worms stuck their heads up from the underground. They were convinced that the chief bookworm had ordered them to attack.

They crawled out of hiding with their eyes casting about for an enemy to attack. They panicked and ran for cover at the sight of their fallen chief. As they hopped for cover, James the third, Crusader of the Second Adam tied his victims in knots, and collected the eyeglasses from all the worms in less than two minutes. James the Crusader let out a sound of triumph and twelve other crusaders flew in to roll the knot-ted worms to the village's birthing center.

Firey sun rays fell like rain from Ecclesia-Don. The chief's body started to melt right there on the spot. James swooped down, lifted Ian from the worm's smoking fist and zoomed back toward the sky. James the Crusader lifted his right hand with Ian tucked safely underneath his left arm. A trail of smoke hung in the sky for a couple of minutes and then followed after them.

In forlorn, I bowed my head in grief for Ian. I began to fear that I had lost him for good. Ian and James the third, Crusader of the Second Adam, suddenly reappeared with the other twelve crusaders trailing him. The youngest crusader's baby blue cape flapped in the wind. The huge *B* on the front glistened in the sun. The baby's name, Eli Ahmir, graced the back of his cape. The baby crusader led the pack of crusaders directly over the books and trees that supported Wormwood Village's existence. Baby Crusader, Eli Ahmir loosened the strip on his diaper, and let the contents fall. The pellets within, completely destroyed the underground tunnel and the cove of trees which had been the birthing center for the worms. Eli cooed with delight at the damage the firey pellets caused.

The twelve crusaders raced to the entrance of Wormwood Village where they combed the area for survivors. It was visible to me that the invasion would be over within a matter of minutes. The baby crusader was on a mission. After the devastation ended, I was left alone with hundreds of worm corpses melting all around me. The worm village smelled of fish and burning rubber.

"I've lost Meghan, and now I've lost Ian again." I spoke aloud to the melting worm corpses around me. After a short time, there was nothing left of the worms' bodies except for their ruby eyeballs. Alone and unafraid, my excursion about the village enabled me to scoop up as many pairs of the red ruby eyeballs as possible. I sat patiently watching the baby fire pellets at work with all the time in the world. Though the fire raged all around me, my body remained unharmed by the flames. The crusader's fire could only hurt the enemies of humankind.

After a while, the fires finally consumed all the worms and began to flicker out. I sat among the rocks, weaving a purse out of dried cocoon slime.

Nearly finished with my work, a sudden thought of Ian and Meghan flashed through my mind. The pit of my stomach felt hollow, and pain gnawed at my consciousness. Their disappearance filled me with turmoil and left me emotionally exhausted. I decided that the only thing that might help would be to exit the premises and continue my journey. My newly hand crafted purse held at least twenty pairs of ruby eyeballs comfortably. I closed the purse flap and hung the purse over my shoulder. I inhaled deeply and walked toward the sunset all alone.

CHAPTER FIFTEEN

Home Sweet Home

My longing for home had intensified since my experiences on the north side of the garden. It would take incredible courage to explain to Mom and Aunt Jen what had happened to Ian and Meghan.

"Ian I miss you." I batted the tears away knowing that crying would not relieve the problem. What was there to live for after all that had taken place? It had been a long, hard journey that had left me physically exhausted and mentally whipped. Suicide was the best and only option since I did not want to be alone.

The more I focused on suicide, the heavier my eyes, arms and legs grew. I tried to fight the sleepiness that overwhelmed me. I jogged in place to carry out my plans. My plans were to commit suicide while I had the courage to do so. Still, my body stretched itself out on the lush grass, and into a fetal position.

Days later, awakening from sleep, the solace of silence washed over me. Somehow, I was comforted in my solitude, and was momentarily glad to be right where I was. The reflection of the sun painted the sky a beautiful hue of golden red. It etched its rays across the sky in every direction. I gloried at the colors that shone on the surface of the river.

The mountains that surrounded the canyon were extremely high and intimidating, but the bottom of the canyon was covered with fruit bushes. The fruit was incredibly sweet. I ate my fill of blackberries, and looked for a place to spend the rest of the evening.

The perfect camp site was on the flat land between the rocks and trees. My reason for that was to employ a quick escape route if I needed to escape from anything. I would be able to scramble up the rock, grab hold of the branch, and climb the tree. I was pleased with my plan, and certain to be safe if anything strange should happen.

Before I could finish that thought, it happened. You know, something strange. Some kind of creature darted out from behind a tree and disappeared behind another. It was extremely agile, and shadowy in appearance, but for certain it was there. My eyes weren't playing tricks on me this time. Here right now all alone, when something decides to stalk me.

Without warning, something touched my right shoulder. In anger, I whipped around to face it. There was nothing there. Then it touched my left shoulder. Again, there was nothing there that I could see. The creature then streaked past me like a bolt of lightning. The strange dark creature pounced on top of the rock, grabbed the tree limb, and climbed the tree. Well, so much for my brilliant defense strategy.

Struggling to locate the creature in the tree, the sun decided to hide completely behind the clouds. This was just great – the sun disappears right when it was needed most. I felt sorry for myself, until I had a flash of insight, and realized that the thing just wanted to play tag.

The creature of darkness drew in more shadows around it, adding more mass to its form so that it could be more easily seen. I ran between the trees in front of me, and looked behind me trying to find the creature. Seeing nothing, I turned around again. The creature was hanging by the crook of its legs from the tree in front of me. It swung back and forth on a tree limb and dangled its arms before me.

Then, it jumped off the tree and lay down on the ground near the rock I had been camping by. Instantly, the rock's shadow on the ground grew enormously. Its shadow spread rapidly across the ground like water spilling from a cup and spreading across a table. Within seconds, the shadow was as large as the rock itself. "What is this?"

The shadow shot high into the air like a jet, and slowly floated back to the ground. It turned white and shrank as it descended, eventually dropping directly into my hand. The white parchment paper in my hand was a letter from Ian. "Allison," it read, "we are having a ball. Get as much rest as you can. Your destiny depends on it. Trust me, trust the Second Adam and trust your Crusader. Love, Ian."

"P.S. - I will take good care of Meghan and Ian." - James the Crusader of the Royal Commander, Adam the Second.

Having read the small print at the bottom of the parchment, evidently, this letter had been delivered by Taven Express. Well, I cared nothing about the Taven thing that had delivered it - I was just happy to receive it.

I sat on a rock and cradled the letter to my chest, ecstatic to hear about Ian and Meghan's safety. A dark silhouette rushed up to me and snatched it out of my hands. "Hey, who do you think you are?" Too angry to be afraid, its laughter made me even angrier. The invisible creature lifted me off the ground, and sat me in a tree. By this point, I was furious and ready to fight. This scenario could have been different if Taven, my personal crusader, had introduced herself to me in more of an acceptable manner.

Of course, there were lessons to be learned from every situation here in the garden. On the other hand, what could I possibly learn from something I could not see? I scooted to the edge of the branch, trying to decide whether or not to jump down to the ground. The mysterious creature held my hands to the branch to prevent me from jumping down. It swung me back and forth, struggling against its weight and strength.

"Let me go!" I screamed.
"Are you sure?"
"Yes!"
"Are you really sure?"
"If you don't let me go..."
"Okay, here goes." I was suddenly falling, desperately dog-paddling in midair.

"Are you crazy?!" My body plummeted toward the ground, and I immediately landed in the arms of the invisible creature. I crossed my arms with indignation, but I held my peace. If I had not, it was liable to throw me over its head, if it had one. I sat there cradled in its arms while it just laughed.

"Put me down, please."
"Are you sure?" Even though the creature was strong, I sensed its femininity.
"You're a girl."
"So are you."

The dark silhoutte shadow took on the appearance of sparkling prism light as she slowly materialized. She was a regular girl, in regular clothes with a big smile plastered on her face. The kindness of her face offset her smile. "Why are you playing games with me?"
"You need to know what it feels like to be rebelled against."

Sliding out of her arms, I stood in front of her. "What do you mean?"
"Well sister, you just got a taste of your own medicine."
"You're calling me rebellious!"
"You are." She never raised her voice nor did she stop smiling.

I saw nothing but fire and in my fury, I picked up the biggest rock I could find and threw it at her. She vanished into thin air.

"Come back and fight, you, you coward!"

"I don't want to fight. You can't win." She materialized again, and grimaced at me with displeasure. I rushed straight at her with my shoulder dropped and aimed right for her stomach, she vanished once again. Taven pushed me in the back of my head, and I swung furiously at thin air, until I was breathless and exhausted.

She reappeared and I lunged at her. She vanished, picked me up underneath her arm and took off into the sky. We flew over the river. "Keep it up." Taven warned.

"How dare you threaten to drop me in the river!"

"It's not a threat. Now calm down or I will have to cool you off."

I held my peace, knowing that she was as good as her word. "All you have to do is listen."

I ignored that and asked, "Where did you come from?"

"The Second Adam sent me." she said, and she fell silent again.

"Why didn't you say that before?" She circled back to the tree. "Well, I might as well introduce myself." We stood toe to toe during my introduction while I extended my hand to her. She was not impressed.

"I'm Allison Milan Flemings and I'm from Farmington Hills, Michigan."

"I know who you are. I know all about you." She turned her head away from the glare of the sun - or was she turning away from me?

"What's your name?"

"Taven, Crusader for the Second Adam."

"The Second Adam really sent you to help me?" She turned away a second time. We sat in the grass underneath the tree in silence until sunset the next evening. I was tired and ready to go, but Taven would not budge.

Instead she leaned against the trunk of the tree, and rested her elbows on her knees to prop up her chin. At first I dared not speak to her, but after so many hours I finally broke the silence. I approached her cautiously and apologized for my foolishness. "It's not as easy as that, Allison. I've been sitting here for hours thinking of what could be done to get you home faster."

"So, what did you come up with?"

She paused for a few seconds, and then answered. "You must take the long route home."

"Why?"

"We have to eliminate that core of rebellion that is still inside of you." I retrieved my place on the ground next to her, without a word.

"Are you hungry?" She asked.

"Now that you mention it, actually I am."

"Good." She spread her cape over the plush green grass, and laid down in a comfortable position to sleep. I stared at her in disbelief, and prepared to spend the night with an empty stomach.

Even with the pain in my stomach, I fought sleep as long as I could to prevent another nightmare from taking place. Not to mention the possibility of waking up with a hairy hand creeping up the side of my face. God forbid that should happen. Nevertheless, sleep eventually overrode my desire to be in control.

Sure enough, I entered a nightmare as soon as I drifted off – but this time it was more heart-wrenching then scary. There were tears in the Second Adam's eyes. He had the saddest expression on His face. God had tried so hard to get my attention – and not just God, but everyone who loved me. My days were numbered because of my bad attitude. The choice was mine either to walk away from the Lord altogether or trust and love Him for the rest of my life.

I prayed until I woke up. My stirring awakened Taven. "You've asked God to forgive you, haven't you? I can always tell when a person has had a change of heart." My smile told the story. It had been a long time since I had talked to the Second Adam. I had spoken with Him many times before, but this time I actually meant it. This time it wasn't to get what I wanted or needed from Him. This time I had completely surrendered over to Him the responsibility of trying to fix things in my life. The weight rolled off my shoulders and rested in His nail-scarred hands.

"Allison, I think it's time to get you home." She hugged me and prepared me for the journey.

"Don't look behind you just yet." I remained facing forward, my back to the rock. "God has placed skills inside you that will aid you in life, and they will help you through your final trial. Make sure you do whatever I ask you to, even if it sounds bizarre to you. The Second Adam's orders don't always make sense to humans."

"What am I to learn from all this?"

"You don't know?" I shook my head no. "Trust in God. Just because you don't see Him doesn't mean He's not there. The Second Adam calls it faith."

I liked what I saw in Taven and wanted to be like her. She was absolute in what she believed. I assured Taven that I would listen thoroughly, and do whatever I could to keep from slipping into darkness. She smiled lovingly and handed me a small wafer. "Second Adam said this is your favorite." I muttered a soft thank you to Him and swallowed the last bit of the wafer, and drank the pomegranate nectar Taven had given to me.

"Now, turn around." Taven's eyes gleamed with joy. She lifted her hand in front of her, as if making a presentation of something. My eyes surveyed the mountain that suddenly stood before us. It was so huge it blocked my view of the sun. I gaped dumbly at a complete loss for words. "Wh-wh?" I muttered.

"It takes faith for this one to come down. Don't you believe that the Second Adam is more than capable?" I gave a smile, but did not answer. Deep down, I did not believe.

"What do I have to do?" I asked.

"Don't say a word until it's time. You just stand still, and look at the mountain."

"Can't we just march around the mountain seven days, and on the last day shout and dance and run?"

"That was for Joshua in his battle against Jericho."

"But it's such a wonderful Bible story."

"Yes, but you are going to speak to this mountain when I tell you to."

"But it's so big!"

"So is your GOD!" She held me by my shoulders. "Do not scream. It is a sign of fear." She opened her mouth to sing. The words floated outward and spilled from her heart and into the atmosphere. She closed her eyes and sang.

You are the dawning of my new day. You give guidance along life's way.

My trust is in whatever you say. Speak to the mountain you say. I will speak to the mountain. I will obey.

Pitfalls in life lift me high, lift me high to higher height. Lift me high to destiny's light. You are, you are my guiding light. You are, you are my destiny's light.

After singing the verse repeatedly, the mountain gave a tiny rumble. Pebbles tumbled down from the mountain and lay at my feet. Taven's voice grew stronger and louder with each refrain. The sun began to set, and I noticed it peeked through the trees that stood on top of the mountain as the mountain slowly decreased in size.

Taven did not know she was being watched by me. Somehow, she appeared taller and stronger than she had before she started singing. It was probably just my imagination. No one could possibly grow that fast. She continued to sing.

The mountain rumbled enough to shake us to the ground. We held onto each other. It was incredibly frightening, but Taven did not miss a note of the song. She was so brave. Meanwhile, I screamed for help almost non-stop. With each scream, the mountain grew taller and wider.

Taven stopped singing. "You were doing so well! Why did you scream?"

She spread her cape on the ground, and served us dinner without a word. "Now what?" I lowered my head in disgust.

"We'll just have to start over."

"But that could take forever!"

"Not if you listen to the Second Adam's heart. He'll tell you exactly what to do."

"Taven, I'm sorry."

"Aw, shut up and eat." We ate and ate and she made me laugh. Our dinner was enjoyable and so was Taven.

Even though it was still early in the evening, Taven wasted no time in bedding down for the evening. "Get some rest. We start over in the morning. Sweet dreams."

"Sweet dreams to you, too." Looking over my journey up to this point forced me to hope for sweet dreams.

Sure enough, they were sweet. My dreams had a sweetness that eclipsed all of my fears. Sweetness so alive, it drew my attention to the smallest details in life. Second Adam's voice rang calmly in my soul. "I love you, Allie." I jumped to my feet looking for the Second Adam. That was the first time He had ever called me Allie, and it took my breath away. His love was so alive; it was felt even in His absence.

The light of the moon hit my eyes, and ushered me back to my place next to Taven. A tiny butterfly escaped from the partially open bag that hung from her waist. The butterfly lit on my chest, and many others followed it. Within seconds, my whole body was covered with rainbow colored butterflies that glowed in the dark. I had learned from Dad that butterflies symbolize freedom, and rainbow colors symbolize covenants and agreements.

Quickly the butterflies lifted off of me and darkness covered me. The butterflies bunched together, pushing and squirming to re-enter Taven's knapbag. I could not tell whether I had fallen asleep or fainted.

A door slam echoed throughout the house. I jumped and noticed I had wet the bed. Baby screams followed the slam of the door. My poodle Charlie stood on all fours in the middle of the bed, trembling. He licked his lip in fear or frustration. My best friend catapulted off the bed, opened the door with his nose, and raced to the laundry room for dear life. I flung my wet undies under the bed, and followed Charlie. Upon reaching Charlie, he had already buried himself in his sanctuary. Dad called it Charlie's Palace. Charlie had buried his head under his blanket.

My poodle pup hated Mom and Dad's verbal knock out, drag out fights. Lately, seemingly so, arguments were the canvas upon which our family was painted. Our pain and suffering were on display for every-one to see.

My eyes darted back and forth beneath my closed eyelids, and my stomach tightened against my will. More memories rolled into my head like a tidal wave.

The sports car pulled up in front of the school to drop me off. "Daddy, are you picking me up from school today?"

"No, I am working late again. But I have rearranged my schedule just for you, Butterfly Princess."

"You are a smart man daddy."

"I have a surprise for you."

"What is it?"

"If I tell you, then it won't grab you the way I want it to."

"You talk funny to be a lawyer, daddy. I love you."

"I love you too. You are my joy." I tossed and turned in my sleep remembering how short the ride to school was. I loved spending time with him.

I gritted my teeth, and a trickle of blood bubbled its way onto the edge of my lip.

I wanted to run, but I could not escape my memories. Taven patted my arm and murmered softly, "Shh! Stop fighting God. Let Him heal you." I continued to dream.

Mom said to Dad. "What do you think happened?" He reached for Mom's hand. She slipped it into his.

"We allowed too many people in our marriage. They looked into our life and saw that we were capable of making it against all odds. So they fought against us."

"Jason, let's fight back."

"Frankly, I think it's too late."

She slipped her hand out of his. "Throw away six years of marriage, just like that?"

"We should have considered the options before we had children." He stammered as he spoke.

"What about our home? Not this house, I mean us, our home, most importantly, the girls. For God's sake, we still love you!"

"Look at you Janet, you're beautiful. Any man, white or black, would love to have you in his life."

"You mean any man except you?" He ran his hand over his neatly trimmed beard.

"Have you ever thought about reviving your modeling career?" I will never forget the look on Mom's face from where I was hiding in the room. She slowly rose to her feet. Mom looked out of the bay window from across the room and approached the window as if it revealed all of Daddy's hidden secrets.

"The truth is you have a girlfriend. As a matter of fact, you have two. It's not that you don't love us. It's just that you would feel uncomfortable here."

"What would possibly make me feel uncomfortable?"

"I've known for awhile that the Lord and I cramp your lifestyle."

"Wait a minute. I love him too."

"You've walked away from Him, Jason. I will never give up God for anyone . . . not even you. Your heart's not here. Since your mind is already made up, you are free to go." With that statement said, in dread, I squeezed Charlie's stomach. It was too late for me to leave the room.

Charlie's whimper exposed my hiding place. He leaped up from my arms to scurry from the room. At that moment, I blamed Mom for Daddy's departure.

"Mommy, how could you?" She reached for me. I pushed her hands away and mumbled. "I will never forgive you for this." I was tormented day and night by those words still ringing in my ears. From that moment on everything I had done in childhood had hinged upon them.

Daybreak could not have arrived at a better time. The sun's warmth settled on my face. Its rays caressed the golden streaks of hair atop Taven's head. She stood to her feet and said. "Let's work on getting you home, young lady."

Once more Taven stood before the massive rock and sang. This time I was more in tune with what was going on. God had cleansed my memories last night, so that my feelings toward my mother would be different. I still had a long way to go, but the willingness to operate in His strength prevailed.

Taven's delivery of her song was as fresh and beautiful as it had been when she sang her first note yesterday. To possess the same inner strength and confidence that she had would be an honor before God. It dawned on me that after all this time, Taven was singing to the Second Adam. I opened my mouth wide and sang along with her, pouring out my feelings to the greatest love on planet earth and the greatest love out of this world.

Taven yelled. "Now is the time! Do it now!" What she expected me to say to the mountain was beyond me. It rumbled and moved closer to me.

I closed my eyes frightened by its presence. "Allison, open your mouth!" It felt foolish, but I had promised Taven I would do whatever she would ask me to do.

Words came pouring out of my spirit. "Mountain of rebellion, you have to move. Adam the Second made it impossible for me to lose!"

The foundation of the mountain shook severely, and it crumbled into pieces around our feet. Trees and rocks slid down the mountain without a flinch from me, even when an enormous boulder crashed past us. A mighty sea suddenly appeared, and swallowed the remnants of the broken mountain. Only a beautiful field remained where the mountain had been. On my knees, I sang to the lover of my soul for deliverance.

There had been so many lessons to learn. I learned that energy was in me because I too belong to Adam the Second. I merely needed to know what to do. I was amazed at His greatness.

Taven strode toward me and beckoned for me. I noticed that I had grown as large as she was now, as I sang to Adam the Second with all my heart. We continued to sing our song as we walked through the flatlands. Taven congratulated me for having conquered my mountain.

Sometimes the way the Second Adam works in our lives left me thinking that He was the enemy of my soul. He has never been nor will ever be a harsh task master. I have learned from Taven that all things had worked together for my own good, to get me where I needed to be. My way of thinking had to change. The Second Adam demands that we make faith a way of life.

"This is where our journey ends." Taven announced.

"I will never forget you, Taven."

She giggled. "Nor I you." We embraced one last time. She stepped as close to me as she could, until we were nose to nose. I thought my heart would sadden after she had disappeared, but instead, my hands and legs tingled. My vocal cords pulsated, and peace flooded my soul. Every care in my world had vanished.

Taven had indeed disappeared, but she had disappeared by melting inside me. My feet were planted firmly on the pathway home, knowing that I had been Taven all along. Buried inside me all this time had been a beautiful, strong, vivacious spirit just waiting to escape the rebellion and unforgivenness that had imprisoned my soul. What had just happened to me must have also happened to Ian and Meghan – their counterparts must have been James and Isabella.

After accepting Adam the Second fully, only now was my heart ready to accept the needed change. Unforgiveness had blinded me from seeing how good my mother was to me. I had always blamed her for Dad's departure but now the truth prevailed.

Gazing upon the landscape one last time, my soul was at peace with thoughts of Ian and Meghan. They were being taken care of no matter where they were. The Second Adam would see to that.

My feet followed the path marked Farmington Hills, Michigan. Before long, I was face to face with myself in my own bedroom. My eyes opened slowly to the voices coming from the living room.

Everything was the same as I had remembered it, except for my mother sitting in the chair in the far corner. The pain from a huge bump on my head made me wince and another trail of pain flashed up and down my broken left arm.

I threw the covers back with my good hand, and eased out of bed. Our neighbor, Mr. Adam Fontaine sat on the sofa facing Ian with Meghan beside him. The back of Mr. Fontaine's head faced me through the crack of the door. His conversation with Meghan and Ian centered around me.

"Do you think she's learned her lesson this time?" Meghan asked.

"She barely escaped with her life." Ian added.

Mr. Fontaine's response shook me to my core. "Getting hit by that car saved more than just her life. If she hadn't been hit, she'd be facing drug charges right now alongside CayLeigh."

Ian pondered this, and said. "Who's to say CayLeigh won't use that against her?"

Meghan whimpered. "Oh Mr. Fontaine, no! Mommy's been through enough with Daddy. She shouldn't have to go through h-e-double l with her children, too!" Mr. Fontaine smiled slightly when Meghan spelled out the word hell.

"Sir," Ian struggled to explain, "the car hit Allison when she crossed in front of it to meet CayLeigh."

"Yeah." Meghan added.

Ian's voice shook with emotion. "CayLeigh was the one who was actually in the car with the drugs and the two thugs. Remember, they said they were going to give Allie a lift...and the driver ran the stop sign as she crossed the street."

"That's right, Ian." Meghan added. "And when he was tested, Mr. Fontaine, the test proved that the driver was under the influence of drugs."

"That's worth something, isn't it?" Ian asked. As hard as I tried, I could not remember anything that had happened that day.

"I'm sure they will question her." Ian ran his fingers through his hair.

"Of course they will. The police found drugs in Allie's jeans' pocket."

"They planted them on her!" Heated disgust elevated Meghan's voice. "My sister does not do drugs!" I crawled back into bed to worry.

"There, there Megh. I wouldn't worry too much. Let's pray." Mr. Fontaine asked God for His favor and blessing in my behalf and said Amen.

"Megh, it's your sister's first offense. It'll turn out okay." He hugged Meghan and headed toward the door. "You two get some rest, and I'll check on Janet and Allie in the morning."

What had I done this time? My homecoming should have been a joyous celebration...it should not be hitting me this hard. I guess it just goes to show that bad deeds always come back to haunt.

Mom stirred around in her sleep, and shifted her legs on the chair she was using as a footstool. I peeked at her out of the corner of my eyes. She yawned and fluffed her hair a few times, then smacked her lips, poured a glass of water and brought it to my bedside.

"Hey, wake up woodle!"

I groaned theatrically, as if coming out of a deep sleep. "What did you call me?"

"Oh, just a nickname your grandmother Rachel gave me when I was fourteen."

"Grandma Rachel Zane!" Pain pounded on all sides of my head at those words.

"Take it easy." She sweetly ordered. Mom fluffed my pillow to make me more comfortable. "I could have lost you during this ordeal." She kissed me again and again.

I was astonished to see just how real my weekend had been. My journey through the garden was still vivid...but it was obvious that I had been sleeping through most of the Thanksgiving Holiday at the hospital. Mom had posted photos all over the dresser that told the whole story.

Mother handed me medication. The pill rested between my thumb and index finger. I simply had to apologize for my behavior. I could not live another moment in the same room with myself.

"Shh." She pressed her fingers against my lips. Don't try to explain anything right now. There's plenty of time for that later."

She put the glass of water to my lips. "Here take a sip." She waited to make sure the pill went down. Some things will never change, I suppose.

"Ian's been here since the accident. Now you relax. I'm going to tuck your sister in bed, and say good night to Ian. I'll be right back." She kissed me on the forehead again and left the room.

Five minutes later, mother stood at the foot of my bed in disbelief. "Allie." She dangled the tattered bag of candy. "You know your sister breaks out in hives when she eats too much sugar. Tell me why you allowed Ian to buy this bag of candy for your sister." I stammered at her with a smile.

The bag of candy dangled back and forth like a clock's pendulum, still hours away from morning.

"Well, it's a long story, Mom." Mom made herself comfortable beside me on the bed to share my pillow.

"Get to it young lady. We've got all night."

The End